THE GOLD RUSH GIRLS

CRAIG MOODY

Visit us at: www.vividimagerypublishing.com

Vivid Imagery Publishing
www.vividimagerypublishing.com

Vivid Imagery Publishing print and digital first edition February 2020

Vivid Imagery Publishing books may be purchased in bulk for educational, business, fund-raising, or sales promotional use. For information, please e-mail Promotions@vividimagerypublishing.com.

Publishers Note: This book is a work of fiction. Any references to historical events, real people, or real places are used fictitiously. Other names, characters, places, and events are products of the author's imagination, and any resemblance to actual events or places or persons, living or dead, is entirely coincidental.

Cover art by Melissa Vespertine
Edited by Stacey Kopp

Printed in the United States of America

ISBN 978-1-7328960-1-7 (Hardcover)
ISBN 978-1-7328960-2-4 (Paperback)
ISBN 978-1-7328960-3-1 (Kindle)
ISBN 978-1-7328960-4-8 (eBook)

*Dedicated to all the lost girls and boys
of the world, past and present.*

THE
GOLD *RUSH*
GIRLS

St. Louis, Missouri
Spring 1850

Ten

HE WAS A TALL man, raised up from the fields of picking cotton. His name was Jeremy Brown, a handsome fellow, with dark hair and eyes and a strapping build from his work on the farmland. He was now in St. Louis, the gateway to the West, with hopeful dreams speckled with gold dust filling his eyes. My name is Meredith, and at the age of sixteen, I was an orphan girl, living with one Miss Daphne Jenkins. I worked in her kitchen and around her home as a housemaid. I never knew my mother and father. In fact, I had only vague memories of my grandmother. Granny had taken me in to raise when I was just a sprout. She passed away some twelve years back. Since then, I'd been bouncing around between homesteads, cooking, cleaning, and taking care of babies. Anything I could do just to get by. Miss Jenkins was my latest mistress. She treated me right. She didn't have any kin, only other servants. She lived in a giant townhouse in the heart of the city. St. Louis was by far the biggest place I had ever been. Growing up in the cornfields of Missouri was a far cry from the crowded streets of the city. The people in St. Louis were always on the move. Since the dawn of the California Gold Rush, the city's population had tripled in size. Most wagon trains formed there before taking to the California Trail and heading west. That was why Jeremy Brown was in St. Louis. It was why we met. He was renting a room from Miss Jenkins, and I was serving him. It didn't take long before he took a liking to me, and before I knew it, I was not only fixing his daily meals, but also sharing his bed. After just two weeks, he had asked me to marry him and join him on the trail. I accepted. What else was there for me in St. Louis? A lifetime of servitude? At least this way, I could share in Jeremy's dream of striking it rich in the California gold mines. I was excited about our adventure, and I relished the possibilities of my new life to come.

The week prior to our departure on the trail, Jeremy hasted his charm. I am not sure if Miss Jenkins was too fond of Jeremy's treatment of me. He showered me with gifts of candies and flowers. Nothing was extravagant nor expensive, but everything was certainly fine and greatly appreciated by me. Of course, I was a virgin when I met him. No boy nor man had ever really taken a fancy to me. Jeremy was the first. Although, this was my first time really being around menfolk. Back on the various farms I had grown up on, there wasn't much of the male breed around besides an ox and cock. Other than that, my life had strictly been in the company of women, so I was deeply taken by the attention and affections of Mr. Jeremy Brown.

The day we departed, I kissed Miss Jenkins's forehead and thanked her for all she had done for me. She nodded, smiled, and placed a small leather coin bag in my hand.

"Keep this for yourself," she urged, closing my fingers over the gift. "Don't tell the man about it. Save it to buy you something nice in California."

I smiled and nodded, tucking the small drawstring purse into my apron pocket.

Later, I buried the coins deep within my sole cloth satchel along-side my second housedress and the broken locket I had inherited from my granny. It was the only thing I had of my kinfolk. I alone was my only kin, but I was now a soon-to-be bride; the new Mrs. Jeremy Brown.

We hitched a ride to the edge of the city where Jeremy had a wagon waiting. It was completely stocked with supplies. Three oxen carried the load. I rode with Jeremy on the front bench, a seat that would soon become impossible when out on the open trail. Once off the padded dirt roads that led to and from St. Louis, the barbaric landscape of the California Trail would make smooth and easy riding an impossibility. Like most, we would have to walk. I was ready for the trail. Jeremy had made no secret of how challenging it was going to be. I couldn't read, so Miss Jenkins would often read aloud the newspaper's countless tales of intrigue and adventure that were reported back from those who had made it successfully across the trail. Nearly two years into the California Gold Rush, more and more interest was building, and longer and safer wagon trains had become available to join. We were to link up with ours just twenty miles or so from St. Louis. I was excited to meet our wagon train companions.

The first day on the trail was pleasant enough. Jeremy had become quiet about midday. I heeded his lead and decided not to say much. He seemed to be deep in thought, and I didn't want to break his concentration. I imagined he was contemplating the grueling months ahead of us. I decided to think about our wedding. We were officially engaged; Jeremy had given me a simple silver ring with the promise to make me his legal bride as soon as we were settled in San Francisco. I dreamt of that day. I saw myself betrothed beneath an archway of roses, a small gathering of newly arrived Californians as our witnesses. The promise and hope of my future as both wife and eventual mother were enough for me to agree to take on the risks and dangers of this journey. I tried not to think about the news of the cholera outbreak that was currently haunting the trail, nor the persistent rumors of attacks from the various native tribes. Instead, I dreamt up baby names, a list as long as my memory could retain.

As the sun set on that first day, Jeremy remained silent. His distance soon froze into a striking iciness. In the short time I had known him, I had never experienced him so disconnected, unapproachable, and downright cold. Little did I know at the time, I was soon to discover why.

I began to wonder where the wagon train meet-up location was as we ventured into the dark of night without so much as a sight or sound of fellow wagoners. A small torch hung from the front of the wagon. I was frightened it would catch the canvas covering on fire. From what I knew, most wagon trains halted at sundown and didn't move again until the first break of dawn. Why were we still traveling? The sun had set at least three hours ago.

Without so much as a single word, Jeremy veered the wagon from the trail and into a section of dense trees. Finally, I summoned the courage to speak.

"Where are we going, Jeremy?" I squeaked, my voice small and dry from hours of complete silence. "Is this where we will meet the train?"

He didn't say a word. In fact, he wouldn't even turn his head to face me. Instead, we traveled further into the dark woods, free of any sound besides that of the groaning oxen, creaking wagon wheels, and frightening night noises of the darkness.

Finally, after what seemed like a lifetime, Jeremy halted the oxen, and the wagon came to a grinding stop. In the blackness, I could hear other animals; more oxen, perhaps. I thought I even heard the single whiny of a horse.

"Get off," Jeremy said plainly, no inflection nor emotion in his voice.

I stared at him blankly, the sole torch illuminating his face in a sinister glow.

"Now," he commanded, the shadow over his eyes concealing his gaze.

My heart was in my throat as I climbed down from the wide wagon seat. In the darkness behind me, I could hear someone approaching. Before I could muster a sound or even turn around, what felt like a fist slammed into the backside of my skull, knocking me to my knees. It was several seconds before I could comprehend what was happening. A pair of hard, calloused hands dragged me through the dirt and brush of the woods. The sounds of the animals grew louder, and the dim vision of Jeremy atop the wagon seat—the same sinister hue veiling his expression—faded from view. Before I knew it, a cold, hard object was clamped tightly around my neck. I struggled to breathe, but I didn't dare speak. I was too afraid. The unknown assailant remained invisible. The next thing I knew, I was shoved to the ground with what felt like other people beneath me. The sounds of the animals grew louder. Oxen. A horse. Then, I could make out what sounded like weeping. Sobbing. I could feel countless arms and legs below me. Not one voice spoke a single word, yet the sounds of crying and what seemed like pain-driven moaning was distinct and clear.

I lay paralyzed for what must have been hours, for when my eyes could finally take in the scene around me, the sun had begun to peek through the thick density of trees.

I was piled atop a tangle of women. Girls. I could sense their skin and feel their hair. In a massive heap we lay, seeming to breathe as one. We were chained like cattle. As the light grew brighter, I could see that we were connected to the back of a wagon. There were three wagons, each headed by three oxen. There was also a single horse. In the breaking light, I could see the wagon I had shared with Jeremy. A strange man and woman were busy pulling the supplies from the wagon's backside. The man was short, cloaked in a wide-brimmed hat and brown shirt and trousers. The woman was heavy and stout. Her hair was pulled into a tight bun. She was wearing what appeared to be men's trousers. With brute force, she pulled the cartons from the wagon and tossed them at the man. It was clear she was in charge.

The short man disappeared, his arms overflowing with supplies. In the hazy light of the early morning, I saw the woman grab and rummage through my cloth satchel, locate my Granny's locket and the coins Miss Jenkins had given me, and slip them discreetly into one of her trouser pockets. She looked around carefully, perhaps ensuring that none of her comrades had witnessed.

I didn't move. I didn't speak. I only waited. I didn't wonder what was happening. I couldn't. It was far too unimaginable for my mind to manage. I only waited. Waited to die or be killed. I didn't know. I simply lay motionless, waiting.

The woman approached. Her face was hard and mean, plastered in dirt and muck.

"Up!" she bellowed, her voice gravelly and coarse.

The pile beneath me began to move and rise. One by one, the girls stood to their feet, the rattling of the massive chain that bound us untangling from the chaos. In a uniformed fashion, the girls lined themselves up. It was clear they had done this before. Each was dirty and disheveled. Some were lacking certain aspects of their clothing. One girl, who appeared to be no older than me, perhaps a few years younger, was missing any covering for her bosom. The sight of her bare breasts was striking.

"Eat," the woman commanded, dropping a large bucket at her feet. Immediately, the chain of young girls lurched forward. Like pigs to a trough, they began to sop up the contents of the wooden pail. I watched in horror as they slapped and scraped at one another. It appeared they hadn't eaten in days.

"Eat!" the woman shouted.

I looked up from the massive feeding frenzy. The woman was looking directly at me, her small, beady eyes locked on mine.

I only stared back. I didn't know what to do. I was too terrified to say or do anything.

"Eat!" she screamed, this time shoving my entire body toward the bucket. I fell upon the backs of two girls who instantly threw me from their shoulders. Landing in the dirt behind the heaving mass of feeding females, I was able to take in the scene more clearly. Nine. There were nine girls—all similar in age, all chained to one another—with the sole chain leading to the closest wagon. Around the necks of each girl was a large, massive collar made of thick iron. I lowered my chin to find the cold sting of my own collar pricking at my skin.

The woman began to approach me, a switch from a tree gripped tightly in her fist. Before I could utter a word or even move, she struck me across the face, the piercing snap of the branch searing a fire over my flesh.

"Eat!"

I crawled toward the bucket and pressed my way between two of the girls. I didn't think. I didn't hesitate. I only moved. Like the others, I began to sop up the mushed food that lay cold at the bottom of the cracked and worn wooden half barrel. The others scooped it ravenously with their fingers. Some even had their faces pressed in the mush. I picked at what I could manage, sliding bits and pieces over my tongue without concern nor the ability to taste. The fire-like blaze across my face itched and burned. I saw droplets of blood sprinkle over the gray mush beneath me.

Eventually, the bucket was depleted, and the mass of girls stood to their feet. I was the last on the chain, a human train that snaked many feet from the wagon. No one spoke as the oxen began to move and the small wagon train jolted forward. I couldn't see Jeremy, although I didn't try looking for him all that hard. The woman was behind me, her gruff and fearsome voice barking over the chain-linked line of girls in a thunderous roar. She had an accent. Foreign. I wasn't able to decipher what it was. I had only heard a few European accents in my time, and mostly only recently during my short time in St. Louis.

The wagons broke free of the density of trees; the open plain of nothingness rolled out for miles. There was no trail. We rode over rocks and dirt. My worn leather shoes provided little padding to the terrain below my feet. It wouldn't be long before they fell apart altogether. The wagon train stopped; a trail was now visible. There was some shouting between the short man and another male voice, which I presumed was Jeremy's, before the train moved again. The wagons pulled out onto the trail, the obvious imprints of other wagon wheels and the footprints of their occupants—both man and beast—distinct beneath our feet.

My mind remained still. I couldn't think. I didn't try to. I didn't attempt to figure out what was going on. I only knew I needed to walk. To move. To follow. The hard footsteps of the woman loomed behind me.

After what must have been hours, the wagon train finally halted. There was a small stream nearby. You could hear it bubbling and trickling in the distance. The short man appeared a while later with an iron pot in his hands. He lowered it, and one by one, each girl was made to drink. The man didn't speak a word as this occurred. Gently, he guided each girl's face to the water, allowed them to drink, and then pulled them back in line with a quiet and methodical movement. He smiled at me as he neared, carefully searching my face with his eyes.

"Time for water, Ten," he said softly. He pulled me toward the pot and lowered my head. By this point, the water was nearly depleted, so I had to practically lick the bottom of the cast iron to satiate my enormous thirst. The pot was moved, the chained females realigned, and the wagon train moved forward. It was dark before we stopped again, once more under the canopy of a nearby patch of trees. During the trek along the trail, I had not seen another wagon the entire day. It was only us: the three wagons, nine oxen, a single horse, which the short man rode on, the large woman, an unseen Jeremy, and the chain of girls. In the darkness, we huddled as one mass, each girl pressed against the other in an instinctual search for warmth. It was several hours of night before the torches were lit and the woman appeared.

The girl she grabbed from the pile began to whimper as the woman unlocked her collar. Without a sound, she was led to the back of the wagon we remained chained to. In the faint light of the woman's torch, I watched her hastily wipe the girl's face, arms, and other visible bits of skin with a rag. Then, to my absolute horror, the woman lifted the young girl's skirt, pulled down her undergarments, and began to wipe the girl's womanhood. She turned her around and did the same to her backside. She eventually exposed her torso and did the same there, wiping each bit of skin with a quick and seemingly rough movement. She redressed the girl and helped her into the back of the wagon. Voices were coming from the other side. The wagons had been situated into a small circle. In the center, a large fire had been lit. I could hear its loud crackling and feel the heat of the flames even in the good distance between me and it. The oxen were grazing nearby, their distinct grunting and chewing nearly deafening.

Strange voices filled the air. There were others here. At least two. I couldn't make out the words they spoke, but the voices were new and unfamiliar. Finally, I heard Jeremy, his voice clear and loud. There was some kind of exchange going on. I imagined it was for supplies or even an ox. The chatter went on a few more minutes before the wagon we were connected to began to shudder and creak. I could hear the girl screaming from within. The woman reached in and the screaming ceased. The wagon shifted and bounced in place. A man's voice could be heard from within. His breathing was loud and labored. The girl no longer made a sound. After several minutes, the shaking wagon stood still. The man's voice was back out in front of the wagon, and the woman pulled the girl from the wagon's backside. Her hair was matted over her face; she was completely nude. The sight of her nakedness in the dim light from the fire was horrifying. The woman redressed her in the same ratty dress she had been in, led her back to the pile of half-sleeping girls, refastened her collar, and moved away toward the others around the campfire.

It was at that moment that my brain finally awoke. It was then that I knew what was happening.

Obey

I AWOKE TO A SWIFT kick in the head. The girls were lining up. I joined them without a sound. The same routine as the day before commenced. The wooden half barrel was dropped, the slop consumed, the line reformed, and the wagon train continued. Once again, the short man explored the nearby California Trail before the rest of us broke from the canopy of trees. It was now clear to me why this was. He was making sure there were no others who could see us. We were meant to follow just behind or just before other trains. We were meant to stay in the shadows.

After several hours of walking, we stopped for water. This time, there was no nearby stream, so water that had been collected from the day before was divvied out in the same iron pot and in the same one-by-one order as yesterday. Again, the short man smiled at me, referring to me as *Ten*. I assumed this was my number in the order of girls. A few times now, I had heard him and the woman refer to other girls by a number, never a name. It was clear that out here, we were a product, stock; a commodity. Our identity and humanity did not matter.

As we settled beneath a new covering of trees for the evening, Jeremy walked near enough for me to see him. Without a thought or a moment's hesitation, I called out to him.

"Jeremy!" I cried, causing his head to turn in my direction. For just a moment, he stared at me with what appeared to be a glint of sadness wetting his eyes. Quickly, though, he turned away, returning to the task he had embarked upon before seeing me.

Again, night fell around us, and again, we girls huddled into a heaving mass. No one spoke, but we waited on bated breath with the same anticipation. Who would be chosen next?

Hours after nightfall, strange voices could be heard in front of the wagon. This time, there was a group, more voices than I could count. My heart skipped with fear.

The woman approached, the glow of her torch red and ominous.

She grabbed me, pulled me to my feet, and dragged me toward the back of the wagon. I resisted. I broke free of her arm and dashed back to the pile. She was behind me within a second or so, angrily securing a fistful of my hair and snatching me toward her.

"Don't fight!" she growled, her accent thick and threatening.

She hauled me by my hair toward the wagon. She tore off my dress and ran the rough and ragged cloth over my body. I tried to resist as she reached my private areas, but she was far too quick and strong. She knew exactly what she was doing. She had a clear and concise method. She unlocked my collar and pushed at me to climb inside the wagon. I refused. I simply stood still and stared at her, every fiber of my being radiating with defiance and anger.

"No," I said sternly, so calm that I surprised even myself.

The woman's eyes exuded a rage I could barely comprehend. I had never witnessed someone so cruel, so angry.

She struck me across the face with the torch. For a brief moment, the end of my hair caught fire. I lifted my hand to extinguish it, but the woman stopped me. She glared into my eyes as the flame crept up the clump of strands, the putrid stench of burning hair filling the tight space between us.

"Don't fight," she growled again, finally releasing my arms, allowing me to put out the flame.

She lifted my hair, pulling it so hard toward the wagon that I had no choice but to follow. Once inside, she shoved my backside so forcefully that I fell onto my stomach. In the faint light from the nearby bonfire, I could see a tiny bed made of straw, the dry hay hastily covered with a ragged and torn burlap sack. I lifted onto my knees and started to crawl back toward the rear cloth flaps where I had been pushed in, when a man appeared at the front side of the wagon.

"Hello," he spoke, his voice low and deep.

I squinted to see him better, his face shadowed by the glowing twister of flames that whirled in the distance behind him.

I turned my head back toward the cloth flaps and continued to crawl, but the woman reached in and struck me across the face. I couldn't see her, but I could hear her voice grunting from just beyond.

"Obey," she hissed, striking me once more.

I turned to face the man, who had inched closer. I could see him now. He was young, perhaps my age or just a year or so older. In another place and time, perhaps I would have fancied his youthful attractiveness, but in the glow of the nearby campfire and roaring fear from within my soul, I wanted nothing more than to be as far away from him as humanly possible.

"I won't hurt you," he whispered. "I promise."

I shuddered, my cold body shaking in terror.

"Come," he urged, pulling me by the hand toward him.

I shook my head.

"No," I whimpered. "Please, no."

I could see a slight look of sympathy in his eyes, but it was soon replaced by impatience.

"Now, look. I've already paid for this here time with you. I ain't got time to play around. We gotta get back to our crew. Daylight is only just an hour or so away."

I shook my head again. I started to inch back toward the back of the wagon.

Before I could move any noticeable distance, the woman crawled through the cloth flaps at the rear of the wooden vessel and gripped my shoulders. Her grip was hard and tight. She squeezed my skin so powerfully that flashes of light danced before my eyes.

"Obey," she seethed, the smell of her rancid breath choking me from behind.

She pressed me down onto the small straw mattress, the harshness of the burlap sack scratching at any exposed skin.

The young man darted his eyes from me to the woman.

"Ya want me to just do my business right in front of ya?" he questioned, his young face confused and almost innocent.

"Go," she commanded. "I hold."

He hesitated.

"I say go!" the woman barked.

Clumsily, the boy undid his trousers and moved forward. Pressing a rough and calloused knee over my face, the woman snatched my skirt up and removed my undergarments. Before I could utter a sound, the boy was inside me, the fullness of him deep and painful.

Although I had shared Jeremy's bed for nearly a week, he had touched me only once. He was caring and moved slowly. There had been no force that night. No pain.

Here, this boy was rough and uncoordinated. He pounded his hips against my pelvis like a mule stamping on a snake. In what seemed like no longer than a minute, he was done, removing himself before spilling his seed.

The woman never lifted her knee. I was unable to see the entire time. I felt her return my undergarments to my hips, lower my skirt, and then lift me onto my legs. I was dizzy, the scene around me spinning in a fire-red blur.

Pulling me by the hair again, the woman jumped from the back of the wagon, dragging my body down with her. With a loud thud, I fell onto the hard dirt of the forest floor. My collar was reattached, and I was led back to my place in the pile. Not a word was spoken as I was shoved onto the heaping mass of sleeping girls. My job was done, and I was left alone for the rest of the night. Another girl was pulled from the mass, her screams quickly halted by the fist of the woman. She was cleaned and thrown into the wagon, with what I presumed was another man waiting for her on the inside. This went on for another hour or more. Aside from me, five girls were pulled from the pile that night, cleaned, forced into the wagon, raped, and then returned to the heap.

This was to continue for every foreseeable night to come.

Cholera

I HAD LOST ALL TRACK of time. Each day was just like the one before it. We marched, we drank; we were fed only once, first thing in the morning, and then piled at night for the taking of men.

From what I gathered, the short man would ride to the nearest wagon train. He would then return with a group of women-starved and excitable men of all ages and creeds. As time went on, I became less and less sensitive to the encounters. The number of men who took pleasure with my uncooperating body blurred and faded with the passing of weeks. Eventually, I stopped resisting the woman. We all did. There was no use. Fighting her only made things worse. It was best to just obey and comply. Doing so meant less harsh treatment, less abuse and fewer beatings.

One night, free of the protection of any trees, we huddled into the tightest mass yet. A vicious thunderstorm pounded at our backs. The woman, the short man, and Jeremy all took shelter within the wagons. Even then, a line of men appeared for their paid time with the girls. As always, several of us were picked from the pile like produce and shoved inside the wagon. When it was my turn, I saw Jeremy seated in the far corner, where he was taking shelter from the ferocious rainstorm. I saw his eyes gaze in my direction as a fat, vile, and smelly man had his way with my body. The man lapped and slopped on my nether regions like a cow sucking on a rare piece of fruit. I glared back at Jeremy with a stone-cold iciness he was sure to feel. He looked away with what appeared to be a faint glint of shame flickering over his face in the darkness.

The next day, we were unchained. Stunned, we simply stared as the woman unlocked each of our collars.

"If you disobey, I relock," she said frankly. "We are far on the trail now. There is no use in running. You will die out there alone."

She didn't need to warn us; the reality of our circumstance was obvious. We had been marching for weeks. We were countless miles from any local civilization. Our only hope was to find one of the nearby wagon trains we carefully trailed or kept just ahead of. But even then, there was no guarantee of salvation.

Now unchained, there was a sense of freedom that fell over us girls. Day by day, as we continued our daily routine without the confines of the iron collars, we began to chat with one another, learning each other's names, ages, and places of origin. The ages ranged from as young as twelve to as old as twenty-seven. Everyone was from some state between Georgia and Missouri. It was clear that Jeremy had employed the same deceitful trick at harnessing us all. He quickly charmed and wooed, promised marriage, and then brought us to the waiting wagon train. I was the last to be collected. As with me, most of the girls were orphans; some were just from desperately poor families who were eager to be relieved of a near-adult mouth to feed. Jeremy made himself out to be such a kind and charming man that I doubted any of the parents who willingly allowed their daughters to go with him could have ever imagined the hell he was now bestowing upon one of their children.

The woman was German. Her name: Agatha. I knew this because the short man often referred to her as "the German bitch"—never to her face, of course—or he would call her by her name when addressing her directly. Agatha was stern and cold to everyone, including the short man and Jeremy. I didn't know the short man's name. Not until much later. Jeremy kept to the front of the wagon train most of the time, and Agatha only referred to the short man with shouts, grunts, or bellowing commands. He never resisted her. In fact, it was obvious he was just as terrified of her as we girls were.

I slowly took a liking to a petite, young blonde named Emma. She had been plucked from her family farm in Tennessee. She was one of the few of us who had received a semi-formal education. Her mother was from a wealthy family, and though she had become a farmer's wife by choice, she shared her gift of education with each of her children, a brood of fourteen.

Emma talked a lot. In fact, she hardly ever stopped talking. Once I initiated a conversation with her, the sound of her voice would echo around my ears for hours on end. I didn't mind, though. It was a way to pass the time and distract my wandering thoughts.

More and more, I got to know the other girls. Emma remained my favorite. I was closest to her, but that is not to say that I didn't find many of the other girls to be kind, sweet, and even charming.

The eldest, Martha, remained quiet and semi-defiant of Agatha. From the whispers of the other girls, I had come to know that Martha had a small child. A boy. Jeremy had promised her they would return for him six months or so after they had settled as a married couple in San Francisco. I think Martha had long accepted the truth and cruelty of her fate. No one said it, but we all knew she would never lay eyes on her boy again.

***

On one particular morning, the air a bit cool, the sky clear and calm, the woman woke us with a frantic howl. Sophia, one of the youngest, had fled in the night.

"Who knows where she is?" the woman hollered, her favored switch gripped tightly in her fist. "Who?"

"No one knows, you old cow," Martha responded. Within seconds, Agatha had reached her, striking her several times with the weaponized tree branch.

"Maybe she was taken by a wolf?" I heard Emma suggest. I winced as Agatha met her with the switch.

"No time for funny!" she screamed. "Where is she?"

No one spoke a word.

"No food until talk," Agatha concluded, turning from the group.

"She ran away," one of the girls piped up meekly.

It was Minnie, a seventeen-year-old redhead from Alabama.

"She went that way."

We all followed her pointing finger with our eyes toward the site of a nearby hill.

Agatha turned and returned to the front of the wagon train. Within minutes, the short man was seen speeding off on horseback toward the hill.

Hours went by. No food. No water. Our general chit-chat soon turned to a starving, parched silence as we waited in the midday heat. Finally, just before sunset, the short man returned with Sophia. We listened in silence as Sophia screamed for her life at the front of the wagon train. We could hear Agatha and Jeremy taking turns beating her, their voices shrill and panicked. It was clear that they feared losing one of us more than anything. We were the link to their survival and the promise of their future.

We had to march in the darkness that night, now miles behind the nearest wagon train. The stars were so brilliant that I felt as though I could pluck a handful of them just by reaching out. There was no moon, only stars. I wished upon them as we marched, praying to some god above to rescue us girls from this endless hell we were living in.

***

We never stopped marching as the blistering sun rose. We marched and marched, too tired, starving, and dehydrated to chance wasting any energy on futile conversation. We did take one short break near a creek. We were allowed to drink, but food was never given. Near nightfall, we could smell Jeremy making his usual flapjacks, their intangible aroma filling the air in an unimaginable form of torture.

I witnessed several girls picking at the dirt that night, pulling roots, shrubs, weeds, and even small bugs to their lips for nourishment. I remained still, the hunger in my belly as wide and endless as the California Trail.

For whatever reason, there were no men for several nights. Perhaps we had lost the nearest train. I wasn't sure, but I, as well as the other girls, relished the break in our forced sexual servitude.

Along the trail, we had begun to travel past countless graves. Just one or two, here and there, fresh mounds and wooden crosses marking their place. Soon, though, the number increased to beyond what could be counted. I saw more graves than I could ever remember seeing in my entire life.

"Cholera," I heard Agatha mumble as we marched past a freshly dug set of cross-marked mounds. It seemed the newspaper stories Miss Jenkins had read to me were true. The dreaded sickness was ravaging the trail.

Eventually, to us girls' collective dismay, the men began to arrive again, always in groups, and always in the thick blackness of night. Some nights, I couldn't even see the men that would lie on top of me, thrusting their weakened passion with pathetic stamina. Unlike the first few weeks on the trail, the men were now worn down and weary. The seemingly endless grind of slow-paced traveling was taking its toll. I wondered why they bothered to take up the short man's offer of purchased sex with females whenever he rode out to the nearby trains. Weren't they more interested in saving their money, health, and quickly depleting energy for the rest of the hard and relentless journey? I didn't understand it, but the men kept coming. Night after night. Night after night. Night after night.

* * *

The first to get sick was Anna, a fourteen-year-old from North Georgia. She had vomited her share of morning mush, and by noon, she had collapsed behind the wagon we were chained to. Agatha and the short man retrieved her, dragged her to the back of the wagon, and tossed her inside. By that evening, we saw Jeremy digging on the side of the trail. We began to weep as we watched Agatha and the short man pull Anna's lifeless body to the shallow grave and roll it within. Jeremy buried her. No marking was left. No cross made. No prayers said.

The rest of us girls, now nine, wept in silence.

Just Six

S OPHIA WAS THE NEXT to die. Like Anna before her, she had vomited her morning meal and was dead before sundown. This time, they didn't bother to bury her. We watched in tearful horror as the short man and Agatha simply dragged Sophia's body to a nearby off-trail ditch and dumped her in it. No one spoke as they moved the caravan forward.

Eight girls now. Eight.

A few nights later, after another lull in the cycle of men, the young man who had been my first forced sexual encounter returned. Aside from the cycle of strangers, the same group of men would often visit the wagon. Some of the girls had begun to form a liking to several of their favorites. Emma even claimed to be in love with one man she referred to as *Pa*.

I grimaced at the notion. How disgusting to love a man who forced himself on you and paid these vile pigs to use and discard of your body. The three evil creatures who headed our wagon train didn't even have the decency to bury one of their deceased commodities. I detested and loathed everything about each of them: Jeremy, Agatha, and the short man. I wished them nothing but destruction; long, drawn-out, painful suffering; and excruciating deaths. I had become indifferent to the men, but I would certainly never find kindness, much less love, for any of the captors.

The young man who had been my first encounter was different. On this night, to my complete surprise, he wasn't interested in fornicating. Instead, he just wanted to talk, and he paid Jeremy for me to listen. We stayed inside the wagon alone for some twenty minutes or so, the maximum time Jeremy and Agatha would allow, and I listened as he spoke of his home life with his mother, father, brothers, and sisters.

His name was Charlie. He was eighteen, a blacksmith, with the same dream as most who were traveling the trail: striking it rich in California.

I listened in silence. I didn't respond to anything he said, but I did find a bit of empathy for him as he vented about his struggle on the trail. In the end, I still detested what these men did to us and how they allowed our captors to use and abuse us, but despite that, I retained a general indifference toward them as individuals.

* * *

Minnie died next. She went in her sleep. None of us had even known she was sick. They buried her, but hardly enough to cover her completely. I could see her distinctive red curls flowing out from the top side of the hasty mound. I stared back at the sight as we marched on, until it blurred from view.

Seven girls remained. Just seven.

Soon, nearly every girl began to suffer from bleeding gums. Some burned with a fever and could hardly walk. The caravan was forced to stop several times during the day to retrieve sick and fallen girls. By the end of that week, only five girls were able to walk behind the last wagon.

No one died for several weeks. The bleeding gums and fever came and went just as the days and nights. The men didn't care if we burned with fever, if our bowels growled and bubbled, or if our mouths stunk of dried blood and disease. They had their way with us anyway.

Charlie appeared one final time. He asked me to run away with him. He wanted to take me back to his wagon train, saving me from my forced vassalage of sex and shame.

Agatha was nearby. She heard him and swiftly removed him from the wagon. I heard Jeremy and the short man load their shotguns as a threat. Agatha cocked the pistol she kept strapped to her massive thigh. I never saw Charlie again.

***

Josephine, a once spry, dark-haired sixteen-year-old with the bluest eyes I had ever seen, was the next to succumb to sickness. She had burned with fever for days, her skin polluted with various rashes and puss-filled bumps and sores.

They left her for us girls to bury. We wrapped her in the sole burlap sack that had covered the straw bed inside the wagon, dug a grave with the single shovel Jeremy had provided, and wept as we covered her with earth and trail-side flowers. Martha led the group in a prayer. At the end of it, she said, "May God allow us to avenge your death."

Just six girls remained. Six.

The Plan

MARTHA WAS THE GIRL I spoke to the least. To be honest, I was intimidated by her. As the eldest girl, she mostly kept to herself, and only made herself known when she openly defied Agatha. Even Agatha seemed afraid of her. While the rest of us quickly, if not immediately, cowered to Agatha's brute force and authority, Martha continued to defy her, some two months or so into our journey.

After Josephine's death, everything changed. Agatha allowed us girls to chat openly during our long and arduous walks during the day. She was often close by, and despite her limited ability to speak the language, she seemed to comprehend English incredibly well. To my knowledge, there was never any talk nor discussion about revolting or escaping. The very idea just seemed outlandish and preposterous, but after we had buried Josephine, the remaining girls began to rumble about such a notion as we huddled in our usual pile once the sun had set and the wagon train anchored for the night.

Martha always led the talks. It was clear taking over the wagon train had been something she had carefully contemplated and planned for weeks. Aside from Martha and myself, there were four remaining girls, all ranging in age. Susie was the youngest, age twelve, a quiet girl from Western Kentucky. Then there was Emma, my favorite, age fourteen. Then me, sixteen; followed by Beth, seventeen; and Caroline, age nineteen. Like me, both Beth and Caroline were from Missouri. Beth had been living in an orphanage until she met Jeremy, who, as with the rest of the girls, had proposed marriage and brought her to the waiting wagon train. Caroline had lived with her mother and uncle on a farm not too far from the St. Louis city limits. Her mother cried the day Jeremy took her from the homestead. Caroline promised to write her, describing every intricate detail of her planned California wedding to Jeremy. If only her mother knew where her only daughter was today.

Martha was the first to arrive at the wagon train. It took Jeremy several weeks to round up all the girls, so she was the most familiar with the inner goings-on of the system. All three wagons were filled with food and supplies. The wagon that was used to bed us girls was emptied out each evening before the male customers would arrive. From Martha's best count, the convoy included two shotguns, one rifle, one musket, two revolvers, and Agatha's thigh-side pistol. The key to our successful ambush of our captors relied on the obtaining of at least one of these weapons, preferably one of the larger rifles or shotguns. We were never near the supplies or weapons. Everything of value and importance was always kept inside the wagons or on the person of those responsible. Relative to securing one of the lesser-seen guns, Agatha's pistol was the most feasible opportunity we had. Each night, we detailed our plan.

"We will wait until she is sleeping," Martha announced as we huddled together in the dark, waiting for the dreaded rounds of selections for time spent with the men in the wagon. "Two of you will hold her down. I will take the pistol. We will kill her last. We need to kill the two men first while they are sleeping."

I shuddered at the notion. As much as I was infused and excited by the talk and plan to end our ongoing nightmare of hellish pain and humiliation, I was also terrified to participate in a round of cold killings. Still, I did agree that it had to be done. We all did. No one spoke of opposition to the plan. In fact, each girl agreed with enthusiasm. It was the first time I had ever seen so much positive energy and excitement within the dwindling collection of sex-slave females.

As with the daily marches, we were no longer chained during the night. We were so impossibly far from any safe refuge that no one dared attempt an escape. Sophia had been the only one, and we had all witnessed her fate firsthand. We discussed the plan every evening for a week. My stomach fluttered with nervous anticipation as we decided upon the night the plan of attack was to occur. Three days from the current night, we would make our move. God willing.

***

The next two days carried on as usual. Hours of daytime marching, a one-time feeding and two water breaks, followed by the usual nighttime huddle. Again, there was another lull in the parade of men. The farther out we got on the trail, the less and less the men appeared. We weren't sure of the reason; perhaps they were running low on money, or perhaps they were too sick and weak to think about expelling their needs on enslaved women. The short man always managed to conjure one or two fellows per night, usually the younger and more virile ones, but the stream of sex-focused patrons had certainly dwindled to a trickle at best.

***

The third day came. I was so nervous that I had to squat beside a trail-side bush or shrub at least six times to relieve the churning contents of my stomach, much of which was nothing but liquefied matter. The cold mush we were fed was becoming less and less palatable. The mixture of dehydrated vegetable shreds, cornmeal, and flour had dried into a rock-like mound of inedible torture. Again, girls were eating from the ground. Any rogue flower, rare berry, or crawling insect had become the delicacies of the American Plains. We even shared the same grass the oxen grazed upon in the evening. On this day, though, I couldn't manage to eat at all. I hardly drank the water that was divvied out to us. It had been at least four days since we had last come across a natural water source, so what was left for us in the iron pot was becoming stale and murky. Agatha and the two men drank from another container. They never dared to share any food or water directly with the girls, perhaps too afraid to risk the disease and sickness that had already plagued their enslaved flock, or the fear of what the sickly men of the nearby wagon trains were sharing with us.

The night came. We huddled. The hours passed. Only one man arrived that night: Emma's *Pa*. We could hear them inside the wagon, Emma giggling in her girlish way. She was still completely smitten with this man, whose face the rest of us had never seen. The men always came and went from the front of the wagon. They never bothered to see where this mysterious stockade of females appeared from. Perhaps they thought there was only just the one girl they were with. Perhaps they thought we were spending time with them voluntarily. Or perhaps they knew the truth but were just too tired and ragged to do much about it. Aside from Charlie—the young man who had wanted me to escape with him—none of the men ever asked about my fate here on this train. I don't think they cared. They just wanted what they paid for.

Emma returned to the huddle, and the hours went on. The cold night air chilled. Without blankets or coverings, we smashed our bodies together even closer, the slight warmth intensified by the friction of our clothing and bits of bare skin. None of us had any protection for our feet. My leather shoes had long ago worn out and fallen apart. The same had occurred for the rest of the girls. Much of the current landscape was matted dirt pounded into the earth by countless wagon wheels, but the gashes and scrapes we all had endured from the various sharp-edged rocks and other debris had eventually hardened the soles of our feet into callused pads. Like animals, the ground beneath our feet was met with painless steps, our skin numb to the quality of earth.

As the night sky turned purple with the first light of the soon-to-rise sun, we made our move. Agatha slept in the wagon used to bed the girls. The two men slept within the circled formation of the wagons or inside one of the supply vessels if the weather was disagreeable. Tonight, both men were asleep beside the dwindling campfire. Agatha was atop the straw mattress of the bed wagon, snoring as loud as one of the nearby oxen. Quietly and carefully, Caroline, Martha, and I crept through the rear canvas flaps; Beth and Susie waited just beyond the front flaps.

I could feel my heart pounding in my ears as we crawled toward a sleeping Agatha. Her massive bosom rose and fell with the beast-like force of her breath. Martha waved her arm, signaling for me and Emma to creep to the top side of the sleeping woman. In the blackness of the wagon, the slight purple of the impending dawn filled the space with a soft, eerie glow. Crouched in place above

Agatha's head, Emma and I stared at Martha as she readied herself just inches from Agatha's feet.

After what passed like a lifetime, Martha lifted her head and nodded. We moved as one. With every ounce of force and strength we could muster, both Emma and I pressed our bodies into Agatha's wide and broad shoulders. Martha lifted Agatha's skirt and fumbled for the pistol. Agatha squirmed and jolted. She was awake. Emma crammed her fist into the large woman's mouth before she could cry out, which would certainly alert the two nearby sleeping men. Emma screamed. Even in the faint light, I could see the blood. Agatha was biting Emma's fist so powerfully that the young girl's blood streamed down Agatha's cheeks and onto the burlap sack-covered hay below. I looked to Martha, who was still searching frantically for the gun. Agatha began to lift from the hay, pulling Emma and me along with her. She kicked Martha, but Martha didn't budge. She took the blows to her head as she swiftly moved her hands beneath Agatha's undergarments. Then, to my horror, I realized why Martha was not finding the pistol. In the soft light of the fast-approaching dawn, I could see the gun dangling by a leather strap from the top of the firmly secured canvas of the wagon. I lifted and tried to jump for it, but Agatha grabbed my wrist. Emma had backed away, coddling her injured hand. Martha eventually succumbed to Agatha's powerful leg blows and tumbled to the backside of the wagon. Agatha roared as she threw me to the wagon floor. With one mighty movement, she grabbed the hanging pistol and aimed it at my head. I could see her eyes glowing in the faint light, her stare still glazed with the dew of slumber.

There was a commotion outside, and Jeremy appeared between the front flaps of the wagon. He darted his eyes around the scene before him before lurching forward to grab Emma. The short man pulled Martha from the backside, while I remained pinned underneath Agatha's booted foot, her anger and rage still aimed down the barrel of her pistol.

Within seconds, the wagon was cleared, and I was left alone with Agatha. I could hear the two men beating the other girls as Agatha pressed her foot deeper into my chest. The screams and begging of the other girls morphed into one ball of sound as Agatha began to pummel me with the pistol. I lost my ability to see as she slammed the barrel of the gun over my eye sockets. Time slipped by in countless waves as the screaming and beatings continued. Eventually, I was heaved onto the ground with the other girls, the sound of our sobbing rising into the morning air.

The plan had failed, and our lives were about to become far more unlivable because of it.

No More

WE WEREN'T FED FOR another three days. We were given water only once. Starving and dehydrated, the bruised and battered group of girls fed on the dried mush that was eventually given to us like a frenzied pack of wolves. We didn't speak as we devoured each and every last morsel from within the cracked and worn wooden bucket. Thankfully, we came across a small stream. Without care of punishment, all six girls fell into the water, soaking our heads beneath the cool ripples for both hydration and a much-needed cleansing. The detestable odor of my own flesh had long become immune to my sense of smell. Everyone on the trail stunk. The men we were forced to be with, who heaved and plopped their thinning bodies over us, smelled no better than we did. The difference was, we were made to collect their transferred filth. My skin and hair contained the essence of the countless men I had been with throughout the last two months or more. This impromptu bath in the stream felt like a rebirth.

Agatha looked on but didn't scream for us to hurry it along or to remove ourselves from the water. Ever since the failed attempt to take over the wagon train, we had been reconnected to the chain of collars, once more dragged behind the wagon like mindless cattle.

We were beaten without cause or reason. Even Jeremy showed himself to us more than he ever had before. The far-off glare in his eyes had darkened into a cold and sinister stare. You could clearly see how annoyed and disturbed he was by our failed mission. Still, we did not give up. We continued to whisper and plan in secret. The only difference now was we were currently guarded throughout every hour of every day. The three captors would take turns watching over us at night, even though we were chained at all hours of the day, except for the rare occurrence when we were escorted to an elusive creek or disconnected from the chain for an accompanied visit to the nearby brush for self-relieving.

Our whispered conversations were now closely monitored by Agatha. She didn't stop us from speaking, but it was clear she was sifting through every single word that was uttered, most of which just contained the mindless chatter we used to help us make it through the grueling day marches and cold night huddles.

* * *

Another week went by before another man appeared in the camp. Again, it was Pa. Emma was taken to the wagon per usual, but before the expected rendezvous with Pa could commence, there was a commotion inside the wagon, and Emma was led back to the huddled group in tears.

"What happened?" I asked, wrapping my arms around the shaking young girl.

"Nothin'," Emma sobbed, shaking her head.

I looked at Martha, who stared back at me. Martha's face was now scarred by the beating she had received the night of the attack. Her once pretty and flawless complexion was now marred and marked by gashes and dark spots that never seemed to fade. I could only imagine what my own face now looked like.

We heard the men shouting from within the wagon circle. It was several minutes before the scene settled. Then, all three captors approached the group of shivering girls. Emma was pulled from my arms by her hair. I cried out but was struck across the face with an unseen object. When my vision cleared, I looked on in horror as Jeremy and the short man held Emma in place while Agatha stomped repeatedly on the frail girl's belly. Emma's screams were muffled by the loss of air in her lungs with each forceful stomp of Agatha's boot. This went on for several seconds before she was dragged back to the pile and left to whimper.

The group remained silent until the short man had taken his night-watch post at the back of the nearby wagon we were chained to, and Jeremy and Agatha could be heard chatting near the campfire.

"What happened?" I whispered, pulling Emma into my arms. In the blue light of the overhead moon, I could see the young girl's eyes rolling around in their sockets. Emma's hand was still giving her issue. It hadn't really healed right after being bitten by Agatha. Now, for whatever reason, she had just been beaten to within an inch or less of her quickly dwindling life force.

"Talk to me, Emma," I pleaded. "Why did they do this to you?"

Tears were the only response I received.

* * *

It would be hours before Emma would speak again. I never slept that night. I held Emma in my arms as the girl slipped in and out of consciousness. Just before the morning routine of bucket feeding and eventual marching, Emma began to scream. The rest of us girls watched in terrified silence as Emma removed her undergarments, exposing a mixture of blood and some unrecognizable inner-body tissue.

Agatha approached, nodded her head, and returned to her duties of preparing the wagon train to move. Only Martha understood what had happened. She revealed her assumption to me while the wagon train braked for one of the captors to relieve themselves in the bushes.

"Don't you see?" Martha whispered into my ear, her lips practically touching my skin. "She was with child. Most likely Pa's baby. They made her lose it."

I didn't believe it. How could Martha know this? I waited to ask Emma myself. The young girl dragged behind me on the chain line, her movement methodical and almost lifeless.

That night, she finally spoke. Martha was right. Emma said she hadn't had her usual cycle in weeks. She just knew it was Pa's, despite the other men she had lain with. When she told Pa, he became angry and started shouting at her. He revealed her secret to Jeremy, who then acted swiftly to remedy the situation. A pregnant working girl was of no use to this party. She was better off dead than with child.

Agatha watched over us that night, carefully moving her eyes over the bunched group of girls with an unfaltering stare. Martha and I managed a few barely whispered words throughout the course of the night.

"No more," Martha mouthed to me after I had tearfully whispered Emma's name to her.

That was all it took for us both to understand. What they had done to Emma was the final straw after a mountain range of soul-breaking straws. We would avenge this.

We would soon try again to be free.

Free

EMMA ONLY GOT WORSE. Her hand turned various shades of red and brown. It began to smell, far worse than the rest of her did. She stopped speaking altogether. Ever since the loss of her apparent unborn child, she changed completely. I began to worry about her terribly.

Our food rations were spotty at best. Our water reserves were gone, although I had seen Agatha taking a drink from the reserve kept for the captors earlier in the day. We marched on, the early summer sun burning at our necks. We hadn't had a male visitor in days. The short man would ride out every night, but he always returned alone, causing Jeremy to shout at him, calling him a failure. The short man never argued. He simply accepted Jeremy's verbal abuse. I wasn't certain, but I also thought Jeremy was beating the short man. I would hear the short man making noises at night; the nights when neither Jeremy nor he was on night watch over us. The noises were odd, almost like they were enjoying it. If I hadn't known better, I would've said it sounded like the short man was making love. But to whom? There were no other females on the train besides the six girls and Agatha, and the noises always came while Agatha was on night watch over the flock of females. Neither

Jeremy nor the short man ever tried to have their way with any of the girls. In fact, the only time any of us had ever been intimate with Jeremy was during our brief and all-too-delusional courtship with him, which was never any longer than a few weeks at best. Since we had been delivered to the wagon train, all forms of affection, even general communication, had been cut off completely. Jeremy spoke to us the least. Our only interactions with him involved the random beating or berating that resulted from one of the more dramatic events, such as our failed attempt to take over the train.

We continued to devise our plan in the blackness of night, often when we heard the captors sleeping, including whomever was set on night watch.

Martha wanted to take down Agatha during one of the day marches, but to do so would be suicide. Even if we were able to force her to the ground—all the while being chained by the neck—the two men would be on us before anything substantial could be done. Plus, Agatha always had her pistol strapped to her thigh, except for when she removed it to hang it above her on the nights she slept in the bed wagon.

Still, we continued to plan. If anything, it gave us a sense of hope, something to live for, and a reason to carry on.

***

Beth came down with an illness. We all assumed it was the cholera that had plagued us a month or so earlier, wiping out so many of our original clan, but she recovered. The fear of illness and death was an omnipresent ghost that marched alongside us during the day and slumbered beside us at night. Even our abductors were not free from the constant shadow of death and disease. Anyone at any time could succumb to the various life-ending hardships that defined the California Trail.

***

It was a usual day, the sun shining brightly above us, the nearby grass fields swaying in the soft early summer breeze. I needed to relieve myself, so I signaled Agatha with the request to do so.

Everything had become so routine that during the day hardly a word was spoken between the girls and our dreaded chaperone. Without a sound, Agatha knew what we needed, even when she would openly and clearly deny us of it.

Agatha nodded and moved to unlock my iron collar. She whistled for Jeremy to halt the wagons.

Together, Agatha and I walked to the nearby brush. I squatted to urinate, and to my surprise, Agatha squatted too. Normally, she would stand a firm guard in front of the indisposed girl, taking care of her own business at later occasions. This time, though, for the first time I could recall, she relieved herself alongside me. As my own stream ceased to flow, Agatha's urinating pelted the ground as strong and heavy as one of the oxen's. Unlike me, who was severely dehydrated, Agatha had enough liquid inside her bladder to keep her in a squat position for what seemed like minutes. I started to pull myself together and rise from my squat when my eyes caught sight of Agatha's thigh-side pistol. It was just inches from me, the brown leather strap and metal gun a stark contrast to the pasty paleness of her large and dimpled thigh. I looked over at the rest of the train. The girls had all sat themselves down, relishing the short break from walking, and the two men could be heard chatting mindlessly at the head of the wagons.

Without a single thought or care of retribution, I reached for the pistol, grabbing and pulling it with ease from the leather strap. Agatha snapped her head in my direction, her heavy urinating still pounding the dirt beneath her. I could see myself in the reflection of her glassy stare, which now radiated sudden panic and fear. She began to jump from her squatted stance, the urine still flowing, when I shot her. I couldn't see where the bullet struck her, but she toppled over immediately. I turned to see Jeremy and the short man rushing to the scene. I fired again, causing both men to halt in place.

A deafening silence fell over me. My ears echoed from the shots. I could see the girls watching in the short distance between us, their faces a mixture of surprise and complete shock.

"Get down!" I screamed, the pounding of my heart now seeming to throb within my skull.

The short man fell to the ground immediately, but Jeremy hesitated.

"Now!" I shouted, aiming the pistol directly at him. They were still a good ways away from me. I wasn't sure if I would be able to hit them if I shot, but the risk was certainly not worth taking on their behalf.

I moved to fetch Agatha's key, which dangled from her belt. I could hear her moaning as I freed the metal key ring and moved away from her. I kept the gun pointed at the two ground-side men. The short man buried his face in the dirt, while Jeremy kept his head up, his eyes fixed directly on my every move. I dashed to the girls, handed the gun to Martha, who immediately returned it to its fixed aim over the men, and unlocked the five collars. Without speaking to one another, we all moved toward the wagons. Martha walked over to the men, her aim now just inches from their heads. The rest of us fumbled through the wagons, searching for the other weapons. Slowly, each girl reappeared with one of the shotguns, pistols, revolvers, or muskets in her hand. We were now fully armed.

"Get up!" Martha screamed, her voice strong and certain.

The short man rose to his feet without a single moment's hesitation. Jeremy only stared.

"Now!" Martha shouted, kicking Jeremy directly in the forehead.

He lifted to his knees, his eyes a fiery, bloodshot red.

"Move toward the cow," she commanded, nodding her head in Agatha's direction.

Slowly, the two men moved to join Agatha, who still squirmed in agony on the ground.

I motioned for Beth to follow me, leaving the other girls to keep aim on our fallen captors.

Unsure on exactly what to do, we managed to maneuver the oxen and restart their movement.

Slowly, two of the wagons lurched forward, with the bed wagon dragging the now empty chain of collars behind it.

I saw Caroline grab the reigns of the third set of oxen and manage to move the third wagon.

Susie kept aim with Martha. We moved the wagons a good distance before they joined us.

Martha jumped atop the short man's horse. We never spoke. Martha just circled the wagon train with the horse, keeping a keen eye on the quickly fading distance behind us.

***

We moved for hours. The sun had long set by the time we felt safe enough to stop. Even then, we were still too nervous and jumpy to enjoy our sudden newfound freedom or access to the relatively generous food and water supply. After an hour or more of settling the livestock, allowing them to graze on the nearby grass fields, mimicking the nightly rituals we had seen repeated for months, we finally allowed ourselves to speak. First, we chatted nervously about how to start a fire. Then, Beth started laughing, causing the rest of us to follow. Then, we cried, clustering together in our usual nightly huddle. We sobbed, tears of relief, tears of pain; tears of sheer joy.

We were free. Without a plan, without a clear moment of intent, we had freed ourselves of what seemed like an endless cycle of turmoil and defeat. I had always assumed and accepted the reality that the only way out of the hell I was in was to die, to succumb to my hunger or contract one of the deadly sicknesses that ravaged the trail.

Yet, here we were. Free women. Together, lost, uncertain, and terrified, but free.

The Native Man

THE NEXT FEW DAYS were some of the hardest we had ever encountered. Although we were no longer enslaved to a group of opportunistic captors, we were still very much at the mercy of the wide and open landscape before us. None of us slept that first night; we were far too terrified that one or all three of our abductors would catch up to us, even though we had moved the wagon train far into the night with a certain buffer of miles now between us. Still, the chance of them catching us was a very real possibility.

Martha led the group, and she was unrelenting about it. We rarely stopped for breaks, and although we were certainly eating more and better considering how things had been just days prior, we were still no stronger or more energized as we had hoped. Martha marched us on faster and steadier than Jeremy ever did. If we needed to relieve ourselves, we did so at our own discretion, but then had to scurry to catch up to the still-moving convoy. Martha wanted as much distance between us and our former imprisoners as was physically possible. She stopped at nothing to ensure this.

On the fifth day after our escape from captivity, Emma fell unconscious. Nothing we did seemed to revive her. Her eyes rolled around in her head; her hand reeked of rotting flesh. We did what we could to clean and wrap the wound, but it only got worse. I feared the inevitable.

On the evening of that fifth day, we saw him: the young native man, trailing us in the distance.

Beth had mentioned something about a man on horseback watching us, but we brushed her off as imaginative or even delirious. The six girls were depleting the food and water reserves far faster than the three captors had. It was clear that the bits of food we had been given were truly the only possible nourishment the abductors could spare. If they wanted to preserve their lives for the rest of the six-month journey—with some four months remaining—they could not possibly feed nine mouths equally, not to mention the stress on the reserves back when there were ten slave girls rather than just six.

We didn't fear the watching native man. He was far off in the distance, but close enough for us to see that he wasn't a white man and that he was alone.

That night, as we sat beside the warmth of the crackling campfire, a feat Caroline had learned to conquer with accuracy and ease, we heard the approach of a horse. Without a sound, we each grabbed our favored weapon, which we kept planted firmly beside us wherever we went.

Taking aim toward the darkness, the six girls waited in breathless anticipation of what was fast approaching.

It was the native man. He jumped off his horse and moved into the dim glow of the campfire. Martha stepped toward him.

"Down!" she screamed, forcing the barrel of her shotgun into his face. Even in the glow of the firelight, his skin shined with a bronze-like copper. He was beautiful, by far the most exotic human being I had ever laid eyes on.

He obeyed, slowly lowering himself to his knees.

"What do you want?" Martha asked breathlessly, her fear obvious and nearly tangible. I knew she wouldn't have hesitated to shoot him had she not feared firing her gun. Martha made it clear to all of us that we should not waste our limited ammunition—only one case of bullets remained—nor should we risk signaling our position to our former captors, who we assumed were following us on foot.

The man responded in a foreign tongue. His voice was low and deep, his words filling the cold air around us with a sort of warmth. Although we clearly could not understand him, there was a calm and peacefulness about him that extinguished the fear we all so overtly shared.

Martha lowered her shotgun. The man hesitated before finally rising to his feet. Slowly, he moved his hands to the small cloth satchel that dangled around his waist. He wore nothing but a large covering that shielded him from the waist to just above the knee. I didn't know for certain, but it appeared to be made of some sort of animal skin. It wasn't leathered like the boots and belts I was familiar with, but it certainly wasn't a sewn cloth made of cotton or wool. It was the most interesting form of clothing I had ever seen.

From the satchel, he lifted a handful of leaves and what appeared to be strips of material similar to that around his upper legs.

He looked toward the bed wagon, where Emma lay unconscious. No one spoke, but we allowed him to approach her. We didn't need to verbally communicate with him to understand what he was planning to do. There was no obvious sense of fear nor danger. Even Martha—by far the most fearful girl of the group—allowed the man to approach with ease. Martha and I followed him inside the wagon, signaling for the other girls to stand a watchful guard.

With quick and concise movements, the man cleaned and wrapped Emma's hand. He oozed liquids from the leaves and carefully wrapped the cloth-like material directly over her open wounds. It took only seconds to accomplish. Then, he moved his attention to Emma's head. He pressed his cheek to her forehead, causing the unconscious girl to moan slightly and move in place. He pulled a small object from his satchel. It appeared to be a container of sorts, made of shell, rock, or even bone. He lifted Emma's head from the burlap-covered hay and poured the contents of the small container into her mouth. She gurgled and coughed.

Slowly, and with obvious concern and care, he gently returned her head to the hay. He stared down at her for at least a minute before turning his head to face Martha and me.

He nodded. Martha only stared, but I nodded back.

"Thank you," I managed to whisper, my voice clogged with a mixture of emotion. I wasn't sure what had just taken place, but I had an internal sense that all would be well.

The native man nodded and scooted past us, exiting the wagon. Without another attempt at communication, he hopped atop his horse and sped off into the night.

The next day, Emma woke up.

Cornmeal and Flour

EMMA GOT BETTER WITH each passing day. Her hand seemed to heal within a matter of hours. Whatever the native man had done to her had most certainly helped. She still didn't speak, but she would at least eat and drink and was lucid and aware for most of the day. By the sixth day after the native man had treated her, she was back on her feet, joining her comrades on the footed march.

The following day, one of the oxen collapsed. We didn't know why, but it was dead within hours. It had been attached to one of the supply wagons. We carried on with the wagon now headed by only two weary oxen.

It rained that night, and a terrible wind shredded one of the wagons' coverings. The next morning, that same wagon lost a wheel. The cylindrical wooden circle just collapsed, shattering into pieces. We had no idea what to do.

Eventually, we salvaged what we could from the backside of the now-defunct wagon. We took what supplies were deemed essential and struggled to fit them into the other two vessels. The extra weight caused the vehicles to creak and groan, their oxen huffing loudly at the added loads. We hitched the now wagon-less oxen to the remaining wagons.

We left what we had no choice but to leave. The now-abandoned wagon faded into the distance behind us as we pressed forth, our radically decreased supply now rationed even further. We were in serious trouble, and we all knew it, though we never spoke a word of our shared fear.

* * *

Two nights later, Martha first proposed her plan.

"We need to bring in some men," she suggested in a firm and decisive tone. It was clear she had been contemplating this delivery for a while. "Just as the short man did, one of us will ride to the nearest wagon train. One can't be too far ahead. I saw fresh livestock droppings all day today. We are close."

"Why don't we just catch up and join them?" Caroline asked.

Martha stared at her for a moment before answering. "We can't do that, Caroline," she replied. "The wagon trains are made up of mostly all men. They will rob and do God knows what else to us. They are worn and hungry just as we are. They will steal what's left of our supplies and take our wagons and animals. We can't risk that. We have to continue business as before."

"No," Beth piped up. "I won't lay with another strange man. I won't."

Martha just looked at her before slowly moving her eyes over the rest of us.

"We don't have a choice," she stated flatly. "At least now, we can trade services for food. I will ride out in a few hours. I know what to do."

I could tell Beth wanted to continue pleading, but she resisted. We all did. Of course, none of us wanted to lay with another strange man, but we also knew that what Martha was saying made sense.

Who knows what would happen if we approached the nearest wagon train as two wagons full of refugee young women? It could be our final demise. Martha was smart to want to shadow the former business plan of our previous enslavement. Only this time, the prostitution wasn't forced, but an understood necessity for survival.

***

Martha left on horseback an hour or so later, leaving the rest of us to huddle in the darkness, our guns clanking together.

After what seemed like hours, she returned; two other horses with riders arrived with her.

Two young men stood beside Martha as she approached the group. The dying embers of the campfire illuminated their faces.

"Choose a girl for each of you," Martha commanded, her voice strong and certain. "My men are just out the back there. We are all armed here as well. Don't try anything."

The young men nodded, keeping their eyes fixed over the small group of girls. I excused myself by moving toward Martha, who was returning to her horse. Attached to the side of the animal were several satchels of what appeared to be some sort of food.

"Cornmeal and flour," Martha stated, seeming to read my mind. "Three satchels each. This will feed us for weeks."

She unfastened the burlap bags, dropping them to the ground.

"And this," she said, lifting a small jug with her hands. "Sour milk."

I smiled. These were delicacies we had yet to enjoy out on the trail.

Behind us, the two young men selected their purchases: Susie and Beth.

Without a sound and with an air of obedience, the two girls followed the young men behind the wagons. The sounds of their fornicating could be heard all around us, echoing over the wide-open plains that surrounded the darkened trail. The men were loud and boisterous, perhaps their first bouts of lovemaking in months, or perhaps their first experience with lovemaking overall. They were young, so it wouldn't be unlikely if they were virgins.

The two men returned to their horses, nodded at Martha, and sped off into the night.

Martha was right. Reissuing our services would be our only way to survive.

Soap

T WICE A WEEK, MARTHA would ride off into the night, returning with eager young men. None were previous clients. All
were new and fresh. For whatever reason, these men seemed far
less tattered and beaten by life on the trail. They were cleaner and
better fed.

Each girl took her turn with the boys. All except Martha. She
kept herself free of the cycle. She no longer allowed the men to
choose the girls. Like before, we were herded behind the wagons;
each girl was then presented to the client by Martha. Martha kept
the cycle fair and concise. Each girl knew when it would be her
turn, so she would prepare herself accordingly.

One of the transactions had involved a satchel of soaps. This
was heavenly. For the first time in months, I was able to properly
cleanse every nook and cranny of my entire body. My nether regions
no longer stunk of the stench of sweat, filth, and excrement. I was
nearly as clean as I would have been had I still lived in St. Louis.

Each girl reveled in her newfound cleanliness. The men seemed
to enjoy it as well. Toward the end of our time with the captors,
the weak and worn-out men the short man would scrounge up
would only pleasure themselves with their faces aimed well above

the girl below him. Now, as during our early days on the trail, the men were more open and adventurous with where they would place their fingers and tongues.

For the first time since being forced to sleep with strangers, I experienced an orgasm. Previous to this, I had only ever brought myself to climax while alone in one of the beds I had been assigned to in the various homesteads I worked at. But here on the trail, with a handsome young man with wavy brown hair and sky-blue eyes that glowed in the starlight, I climaxed hard and furiously. I wasn't ashamed to realize that I enjoyed this encounter. In fact, I think the other girls were allowing themselves some enjoyment in the sexual escapades as well. Perhaps it was the tone that now set our services. No longer were we forced to engage in what we once saw as filthy and disgusting. We were now working for our own personal survival, without the survival of those who had been taking advantage of us attached to it. Also, the trading had brought us better food, soaps, clothing, cloths, and various other items we hadn't seen since departing civilization. The possibilities of gain somehow infused the wicks of our sexual desire.

* * *

Weeks passed and we worked the plains like machines. Night after night—more than twice a week now—Martha brought the men, many of them returning for repeat visits.

The goods rained in, and the overall morale of the group improved tremendously.

Even Emma, who still would not speak, performed her duties with willful vigor. She seemed to enjoy the new clothing on her back and fresh soaps she could wash herself with.

Life had become as livable as it had ever been for us since our time on the trail had begun.

Of course, this didn't last for long.

Ox Duty

EACH NIGHT, ONE GIRL was assigned to ox duty. We took turns, although Martha would often skip a girl's turn based on the men she secured from the nearest train. Some of the repeat visitors requested the same girl over and over again, so that girl's night on ox duty would be skipped if one of her clients requested her.

It was my night on ox duty. Per usual, I led the oxen to the nearest grass. Unlike our horse or the mules some other travelers used, the oxen would feed on the poorest of grasses. I was often amazed at how easily they would mow the nearest grass patches, finding what leftovers the livestock of the nearest trains had left behind. We were fortunate to have only lost one ox thus far. It was common for many trains to lose several by this point in the trip. Some three months into our journey, and we still had the majority of our livestock. If only the same could be said of the girls.

***

I gazed upon the stars as the oxen silently fed nearby. In the distance, the warm glow of the campfire provided the only light on the vast and open plain. There was no moon, only countless brilliant stars.

I found myself slipping away into my thoughts. I was amused at how content I had become. Perhaps it was true happiness, or perhaps it was just a subconscious relief that I was still alive, still relatively healthy, but most of all, free of our previous oppressors. I tried not to think too much about them, though I did wonder where they were. Had they been rescued by a passing wagon train? Were they trying to catch up to us? Did they turn back and return to St. Louis? I know we all wondered about it, but no one spoke of them. There was an unspoken air of superstition regarding the mention of their names. It was as if the very reference of one of them would somehow conjure their appearance, much like some devil summoned by a witch's spell.

My eyes remained transfixed on the sea of night sky above me, my thoughts lost to their own sinking—until I heard the screams.

Jumping to my feet, I raced toward the nearby parked wagons without thought or consideration of any danger. As I neared the backside of the first wagon, I saw the other two wagons lurch forward, joining the set of horses the night's men had ridden in on.

I heard gunshots, several at a time. All five girls were firing at our moving wagons, even Emma.

It didn't take me long to realize what had just happened. We'd been robbed; two of our wagons were now being pulled away into the night.

They vanished within minutes. Headed by horses, they moved far faster than the usual speed of the oxen.

"What happened?" I asked once the wagons had moved completely out of sight.

The remaining girls scurried around like panicked hens.

"Two men arrived while we were with the others. There was a man for each of us," Beth explained breathlessly. "They hooked up their horses and pulled off with the wagons. Only the bed wagon remains. They took everything. Our food. Our supplies."

"Where were you?" I asked, turning to face Martha. It was her duty to oversee the security of the working girls. How had these men been able to approach and hook up horses without being noticed?

My question silenced the other girls. Together, we stared at Martha, who stood still, her shotgun still aimed toward the darkness the wagons had disappeared into.

"Martha?" I asked when she failed to respond.

"I fell asleep," she answered quickly, never taking her eyes from the darkness before her. "I couldn't help it. I've been so tired lately. It was only for a few moments."

"But enough time for them to steal two of our wagons," I said in a huff. I could sense that the other girls shared my frustration, but they didn't utter a word. We were all still intimidated by Martha, especially now that she was our undeclared leader. But this travesty overtook any fear I had of the eldest girl in the group. My shock and disappointment spoke freely.

"What are we going to do now, Martha?" I asked calmly, a wealth of emotion bubbling just under the surface of my collectiveness.

"We carry on," she finally replied, slowly moving her focus over the group of armed females. "We still have the oxen. We can still move on."

"But most of our food was in those wagons, Martha. The bed wagon only has—"

"I know what's in the wagon, Meredith!" Martha snapped. "Get the oxen. It's time to move."

No one questioned her further. Daylight had yet to break, yet we were going to start moving forward anyhow. The decision felt based more in shock and fear and less in genuine thought of survival.

Perhaps Martha assumed we could catch up to the thieves, but we all knew that was impossible.

Following Martha's orders, the rest of the group resituated the oxen—all eight now attached to just one wagon—a single wagon that failed to include our water supply, cooking utensils, or main source of dried foods. We were going to starve to death, and we all knew it.

The silence that befell the group for hours was the slow acceptance of the new inevitable.

The Natives

THE NEXT THREE DAYS should have killed us, but somehow, we still survived. We found a water source, a small, hardly moving stream, but it provided enough water to satiate our thirst. We collected as much of it as we could, relying on the one iron pot that remained on the convoy. The dried food, flour, cornmeal, even the few slivers of dried beef, had all disappeared with the stolen wagons.

Martha remained quiet for days. She finally relinquished her silence into a fit of vented rage.

"I should have killed them!" she screamed into the heavens, far more to herself than to any of us. "I should have killed them when I had the chance!"

We weren't sure if she was referring to the men who had stolen our wagons or the three captors. Either way, no one interrupted nor responded to her. Conscious of our vanishing mortality, we reserved our diminishing energy reserves for the endless traveling Martha continued to impose upon us. I thought we should remain in one place with the hope a wagon train would soon catch up to us. Martha insisted we keep moving, perhaps still too afraid Jeremy,

Agatha, and the short man were still hot on our trail—if they ever had been at all.

As night fell over that third day, we finished off the last bit of supplies we had for flapjacks. It would be the last semi-civilized sustenance we would have. Each girl picked at her flapjack in complete silence.

As the night wore on and the fire faded, we each fell into our own personal escape of slumber. Our horse had been taken along with the wagons, so there was no way to ride out to the nearest wagon train. That meant no men, no trading, no food. Nothing.

***

I was awakened by the sound of mumbling and shuffling. I could hear a horse flapping its lips. I jumped to my feet, securing my pistol in hand.

It was the native man, the same one who had visited us weeks prior. He was standing over the group of still-sleeping girls, his face slightly illuminated by the dying embers of the long-extinguished campfire. By his side stood another native man, similar in height and age. They spoke to each other in the same strange tongue the man had used when he had first visited our caravan to help Emma.

Only I was awake. Even Martha was fast asleep on the ground nearby.

The first native man saw that I was alert. The two men stopped speaking and stared. I wasn't afraid, but I was conscious to keep my pistol firmly in hand.

The first man reached into his satchel, the same animal skin-covered one he had on him the last time. This time, he pulled out a small skin-covered wrapping. He leaned forward and placed it on the ground close to my feet. I stared for a long moment before reaching forward to retrieve it.

Meat. It was meat—warm to the touch and fresh to the tongue. I devoured it in one quick gulp. My eyes watered at the wondrous flavor. I looked up at him, tears welling in my eyes.

He nodded an unspoken understanding of my gratitude. Both men reached into their satchels, retrieving more of the same skin-wrapped contents. They placed them on the ground and retreated into the early dawn.

I crawled forward and snatched open the small wrappings, each containing more food: meat, grains, and some sort of vegetables. Resisting the temptation to devour it all myself, I woke the sleeping girls and shared what had been left for us. No one asked where it had come from. Each girl eliminated their portion of the share in mere seconds. We were far too starved and malnourished to even care where this manna from heaven had appeared from. It could have been poisoned for all we knew, but we didn't care. Our bodies overpowered any form of rational thought or assumption, forcing us to simply feed and consume.

It wasn't until the sun had begun to peek over the flatlands of the open prairie that we saw the two native men, waiting and watching nearby from atop their horses. The first man nodded, signaling us to follow. Even Martha obeyed the unspoken command. We each gathered our weapons, situated the oxen, and marched forward, following the two elusive natives off the trail and into the hills.

***

After at least an hour of walking over the rough landscape of rocks and grass, we finally arrived at a village composed of strange dwellings made of wooden branches and animal skins. Women and children flocked between the various structures. The smell of cooking meat filled the air. Lines of crops surrounded the dwellings.

The two men stopped our wagon and jumped down from their horses. With a swift gesture, the first native man—the one who had helped Emma some weeks back—led us into the village. Each girl remained silent as we walked into this alien land.

The native people stared at us curiously as we followed the two men. I saw one woman glaring as we neared one of the fires. I got the overwhelming sense that not everyone here was happy or welcoming of us.

The men sat us near the fire, quickly retrieving various chunks of meat from over the open flame. More vegetables and grain were passed around. Again, the group of six girls ate in silence, more grateful than fearful. I looked back and saw several natives surrounding our oxen, hydrating and feeding them. Some of the children squealed with excitement as they bounced around the massive animals, perhaps their first time ever seeing an ox.

We were given water as we finished off the delicious food. We weren't aware of what we were eating, we just ate, but each morsel fired our taste buds to life, taste buds that had been dormant for months from the assault of bland and tasteless mush and dehydrated tidbits. Now, a feast of fresh, exotic meats sizzled through our lips with various unknown vegetables accenting the spice with a new and unique flair. I don't think I had ever consumed food as wonderful as this.

One of the native women approached. She was older than many of the rest. She spoke to us in the same strange tongue, motioning for us to follow her. She led us through one of the nearby crops, which eventually opened to a rippling stream. Without further motioned instruction, we removed our filthy clothing and fell into the water, the first bath any of us had in at least two weeks. I could feel the dirt and stench lift off me as the cool water flowed around my naked skin. The elderly native woman shooed away some curious teenage native boys who suddenly appeared from the towering green of the crop. They giggled as they disappeared back into the swaying grass.

Two other native women joined the elderly woman in washing our clothing. Together, they chatted amongst themselves as they dipped and scrubbed our filthy dresses in the purity of the fresh water. They beat the garments against the nearby rocks, obviously amused at what was in their hands. I imagined they were not used to handling the clothing of white people. Many of these natives were perhaps viewing white people—especially white females—for the first time in their lives. From what I knew, most wagon trains feared and avoided natives at all costs. The myths and tales of murderous, savage Indians haunted the trail like the various illnesses. Most travelers would've rather faced unseen cholera than even one native.

Yet, here we were, naked and vulnerable as three native women washed our clothing. We didn't need to speak to them to understand their intention. It was clear these native people were trying to help, not harm us.

We were provided animal skin coverings as our worn and weathered clothing dried in the sun. We huddled together, grateful for the food in our bellies and clean skin beneath our borrowed coverings. The women retreated into the crop, leaving us alone on the bank of the small yet powerful stream.

In an hour or so, they returned, signaling for us to retrieve our partly dried garments. They watched in amusement as we shuffled into our tattered undergarments and worn-out dresses. We were allowed to keep the animal skin coverings as we followed the women back into the village. Again, the entire tribe eyed us cautiously as we were escorted back beside the fire. The powerful flame radiated a massive whirl of heat. We inched as close to it as we could, enjoying its comforting warmth as it accelerated the drying of our still-damp clothing. We remained there for hours, until the native man—the first we had ever encountered—approached from behind.

He nodded and smiled. His golden skin gleamed in the afternoon sunlight, and his dark hair flowed wildly over his shoulders. He was the most exotic yet most beautiful man I had ever seen. I couldn't help but just stare at him. We all did. Each girl kept her eyes locked on the man as if viewing some mythical creature from a campfire tall tale.

He began to speak to us, his voice booming and deep. We didn't know what he was saying, but his inflection and tone signified a warm and comforting sense of security. He nodded as he departed, locking eyes with Emma. She smiled, the first time I had seen her smile in months.

We Have to Leave

THAT NIGHT, WE WERE led to a small hut made of wood and animal skin. Surprisingly, it was warm inside. We were provided coverings made of various animal furs. We huddled together in our usual cluster, although now, unlike on the trail, each girl was wrapped securely in her own fur blanket. We slept better that night than we had in months. I didn't open my eyes again until morning.

***

Not long after the sun had risen, the native man fetched us from the hut. He led us back to the fireside for food. Again, I saw several of the native people eye us cautiously as we passed them. Not everyone here had the same comforting warmth as the few natives who were clearly working to help us.

After we had finished eating, the native man returned. He smiled and touched Emma's cheek, causing a nearby native woman to fly into an apparent rage. She yelled at the man in their foreign tongue, darting her eyes over us girls with obvious disdain. The man allowed her to finish before replying. Gently, he removed his hand from Emma's cheek and moved to collect the still-ranting woman. He led her away, her angered words still showering over us.

***

Later, the same elderly woman who had helped us to the stream the day before summoned us to follow her and some of the others into the nearby crops. We were given large woven baskets made of some sort of dried husk and shown how to pull the contents of the crop from the stalk. We did so diligently, each girl filling her basket quietly and with contentment. We truly were grateful for the salvation. Surely, we would have perished within a day or so had we remained on the trail. Our time here in the native village was not only needed, but also essential for our survival. Each girl seemed to know that and worked hard at never causing any sort of trouble. Also, the quiet stares of many of the natives were unnerving and suspicious. We were either treated with forthcoming and obvious gentle warmth and clear friendliness, or we were glared upon with clear distrust and discontentment. The woman who had yelled at the native man watched us from nearby. She too was fast at work plucking the bounty of the crop into her basket, but she was careful never to lose sight of the group of strange white females that now permeated her village.

***

That night, we were joined by the natives as we consumed a meal together. We smiled and nodded at those who smiled first, but looked away from those who kept their locked stares frozen over us. The same young native man sat beside us. Again, he focused on Emma, taking bits of his own food and handing them to her.

The group fell silent as the same young native woman shouted over the voices of the crowd. Quickly, she approached the native man, who was squatted next to a seated Emma, and pulled Emma by the hair toward the fire. The man jumped to his feet and struck the woman, causing her to fall to the ground. Several native women moved to assist her, while the native man gently attended to a clearly shaken Emma.

Everyone stared, and no one spoke for several minutes. Finally, the natives began to chat amongst themselves. I turned toward Martha.

"This is going to be trouble," I whispered.

Martha didn't respond; she continued to eat in silence.

"Martha," I whispered, louder this time.

"We have to leave," she eventually replied, never looking away from the food that lay before her. "We will discuss it tonight."

I didn't say another word. I finished off my meal and waited for our escort to the hut. The night wore on, and the natives became livelier and more vocal. They laughed, danced, and even sang. Their native tongue was mysterious yet beautiful. Of course, I never knew what they were saying, but the sound of their voices filled the air in a melodic song that soothed my racing thoughts and calmed my anxious brain.

After what must have been hours, the native man motioned for us to follow him to the hut we had slept in the night before.

Martha waited until the man had left us before addressing the huddled group of girls.

"We've been well fed," she started, lifting her voice above the still-lively natives who continued to congregate around the nearby fire. "We will leave in the morning."

There was some groaning, which Martha quickly halted.

"We can't stay here," she fired. "We don't know what these savages want with us. For all we know, they are fattening us up to eat us. Have you thought about that?"

The notion seemed ridiculous at best, but in the various stories we had each heard from the newspapers back home, Jeremy, or even from each other, we couldn't quite feel secure in the knowledge it was complete hogwash. Martha could be right. The helpful kindness could very well be a clever rouse to take down our defenses, opening us up to the vulnerability of death and perhaps cannibalistic consumption. I shuddered at the thought.

"I will wake everyone up at first light," Martha concluded. "Try to sleep as much as you can. Tomorrow will be a very long day."

I didn't sleep at all. I lay awake the entire night, fearfully ruminating on what tomorrow would bring. Sure, we were well fed now, but what about tomorrow night and the night after that? I think many of the girls felt the same.

For hours, we all tossed and turned, nowhere near as still and peaceful as we had been the night before.

Emma's Farewell

Martha woke us an hour or so before dawn. I was awake already, but many of the girls had eventually faded to sleep. We exited the hut and made our way to the wagon. The oxen were grazing nearby. No one appeared to be watching them, but they didn't wander off. They remained grouped together, foraging on the thick and rich grass of the meadow.

As quietly as possible, we ushered them together and reconnected them to the wagon. They didn't hesitate nor resist. By this point, the oxen were more than acclimated to their life of grueling laborious servitude.

In the faint light of dawn, we moved the wagon forward and back toward the trail. Moving by faint memory, we retraced the way we had been led into the village.

After a half an hour or so of walking, we could see the worn wagon tracks in the distance. We would be back on the trail, heading west, before the morning sun had fully risen.

We heard galloping behind us. The native man was fast approaching.

He looked concerned as he closed in on the wagon and marching girls. He motioned at us, most likely beckoning for us to return to the village with him. We shook our heads but did not speak. Silently, we made it clear of our intention. We were returning to the trail. There would be no stopping us.

Then, Emma jumped from her place in the march.

"I want to stay!" she announced, the first words she had spoken in weeks.

Martha halted the wagon and we all stared at Emma. Even the native man, still perched atop his horse, was silent.

"I don't want to go out there anymore," she declared, pointing toward the nearby trail. "I don't want to be with the men. I don't want to suffer and starve and be humiliated over and over."

Slowly and methodically, she moved her eyes over each girl's face.

"I don't want to die with you," she concluded.

No one tried to stop her as she moved toward the native man's horse. She reached for him, and he scooped her up with one arm, placing her in front of him on the horse.

"Emma!" I finally shouted, emotion catching in my voice.

"Goodbye, Meredith." Emma smiled. "God be with you."

Her words seemed exclusive to me. For whatever reason, she didn't seem to want to acknowledge the other girls as the native man circled the horse around the wagon, perhaps giving us one last opportunity to turn around and rejoin them in the village.

Martha hollered for the oxen to move. Obeying the command, we guided the massive animals as they dragged the sole withered wagon back onto the trail.

I peered over my shoulder, watching Emma and the native man disappear beyond the distant hills.

I knew I would never see Emma again.

Susie's Final Cry

WE MARCHED FOR DAYS, tired, starving, and thirsty. No one spoke very much as the days morphed into nights, followed by yet more grueling days.

We didn't see any other wagon trains. I secretly hoped we would. I didn't care about the danger another train presented; I was tired of being alone with these girls, tired of the same hopeless routine, and most of all, tired of Martha.

No one said it, but I think we collectively began to regret our decision to follow Martha back out onto the trail. A part of me would have much rather been murdered and eaten by the natives than die the emaciated and horrible death that surely awaited me here on the trail.

"I don't think they were going to harm us," Beth whispered to me as we braked for water, the same stale water we had from before our stay with the natives. "I wish we would have just stayed."

I nodded but didn't speak. Martha was always nearby, always listening.

***

That night, as we lay beneath the diamond-like canopy of stars, Susie, the youngest, could be heard sobbing. No one moved to comfort her. We listened as her crying echoed out into the darkness, her heaving sobs bouncing between the sounds of the night.

When we awoke, Susie was dead. No warning. No obvious sickness. She was cold, her skin blue. She had been gone for hours.

We were in a stunned stupor as we buried her. No one prayed. No one cried. We covered her over with the hard dirt of the dried grassland and returned to the wagon.

No one spoke again for several days.

Enough

ANOTHER ONE OF THE oxen collapsed a few evenings later. Martha shouted at us to fetch it water. It was too late. Much like the ox we had lost some weeks back, the poor creature moaned in agony as it took its final breaths. An hour or so later, it was dead.

I had enough.

"This is lunacy, Martha," I stated calmly. "We shouldn't have left the natives. We will die here. We will die out here in a matter of days."

Caroline and Beth just stared. I stood directly in front of Martha, who remained atop the wagon bench.

"Let's go back," I said, more as a command than a suggestion.

The tension in the air had become thick and palpable.

"We march on," Martha replied hoarsely. "Unhook the ox. Let's get going."

"Enough with you!" I heard myself scream, my voice echoing around the few trees that surrounded us. "We are marching toward our own deaths!"

Martha only stared.

"Please, Martha," I heard Caroline squeak. "Please, let's go back."

"I agree," Beth eventually chimed in, her words secure behind Caroline's and my lead.

"March!" Martha screamed, lifting from the seat and aiming her shotgun at us. "We will march. Do as I say!"

Beth, Caroline, and I glared at Martha for what felt like hours before finally obeying the gun-driven command. We marched and marched. We marched until we could march no more.

Caroline fell first, followed by Beth. I dropped to my knees beside them. I looked up at Martha, expecting her rage and scorn, but was surprised to see her weeping, her face scrunched in a hopeless expression, dehydrated tears streaking the dirt on her skin.

We were alone, lost, starving, and soon to be out of water. Death crept alongside us closer than it ever had before.

I knew that soon we would all be taking our final breaths together.

The Saints

WE DIDN'T MOVE FOR days. Four dying girls simply lay on the ground where they had fallen, too weak to move an inch. I slipped in and out of consciousness, only slightly aware that the sun had come and gone several times.

I was the last to awaken when the wagon arrived—a wagon with two men, Jacob and Abraham, who called themselves *Saints*. They were the lead wagon of a train of ten. The other wagons were an hour or so behind them. According to Jacob, these two young men often moved ahead of the rest, which included women and children, to secure the way. The two men tended to each girl, ensuring her allotment of fresh water, a generous helping of dehydrated meat, even some hardtack, which had to be soaked in water in order to consume. Jacob even shared his own helping of rice and beans. As with the natives, we ate in silence, each girl grateful for the unexpected feeding yet still too weak to exert much energy on speaking.

"The rest of our train should be here within the hour," Jacob announced, sitting next to me on the ground. He was tall, handsome, and young. He had wavy brown hair and clear green eyes. I found myself to be a bit shy and quiet around him; that is, once I had recovered enough from my dehydration, hunger, and exhaustion to even notice his appearance.

"We are headed to Deseret," he continued. "Our people have been migrating there."

I wasn't quite sure what he meant by *his people* or the self-reference to *Saints*, but I assumed it was something religious. I only listened; I didn't want to appear rude by questioning anything.

"You aren't the first we have found stranded along the way. We picked up a few others some several weeks back. This trail is deadly, more and more so as we travel along. I am glad we came upon you girls in time."

I smiled and nodded, taking another large gulp of cool water from the tin cup I had been given. I moved my eyes over the other three girls. I couldn't believe there were only four of us now. What started out as ten strong, healthy females had died and dwindled to just four ragged souls, hardly clinging to life.

Abraham was quiet. Like Jacob, he was tall and handsome. He had a large, full beard that covered much of his face, but the same clear green eyes as Jacob. I assumed they were brothers. Jacob, who was pretty chatty, might have mentioned that they were, but I was only half listening to him most of the time.

Martha was quiet as we fed. She hardly even lifted her eyes from her small plate of food. I didn't bother trying to speak to her. I would have preferred she stay quiet forever. I knew Beth and Caroline felt the same. If there was one thing for certain, I was not going to follow Martha's lead any longer. I didn't care if that meant trekking the trail alone. I would have rather died on my own accord than under the reckless eye of Martha.

Jacob continued to tell the tale of his wagon train's journey from Illinois. Like us, they had been on the trail for months. Much of his train included his direct family, some neighbors, and a handful of strangers they had rescued from the trail. According to him, they had only lost two in their convoy, both to cholera, which was by far the most deadly and prolific killer on the trail.

***

An hour or so later, the rest of the boys' train could be seen approaching over the horizon. Given the vast openness of the plain, we could see them for miles before they finally arrived.

As soon as the first wagon neared, Jacob and Abraham approached them. An older man headed the first wagon. He looked a lot like the boys, so I assumed he was their father. An older woman sat beside the man, most likely the man's wife and the mother of the boys. Children started to appear from the sides of the wagon, moving from the wagons that trained behind the first. It was striking to see the children. I hadn't seen anyone younger than the age of twelve in months. To my surprise, these people all appeared healthy and well-fed, especially considering the challenges of their journey. It was clear they had been far more prepared for the trip than our captors had been. From just the bit of food we were given, it was evident the quality and richness were far superior to anything we had found in the wagons after overtaking our kidnappers. Even they had not fed so well.

The wagons continued to line up, braking behind the first. Women, men, and children of all ages slowly migrated toward us, taking in the sight of the newly discovered group of malnourished travelers. It was clear that most were surprised to see four females stranded alone on the trail. Most wagon trains were compiled of nearly all men. It was rare to see women accompanying their men. This wagon train appeared to be the exception. Again, I believe it was due to their trek to what they referred to as *Deseret* rather than to the gold mines of California.

Slowly, each girl was escorted to a wagon that could host her. I was seated next to the couple I believed to be Jacob and Abraham's parents. They didn't say too much to me as the train resituated and redeployed its movement. The boys initiated their oxen, and the rest followed suit. The bumpy ride atop the wagon bench was rough and uncomfortable but sure beat walking beside the oxen. The train moved for hours, finally settling just before sundown. Systematically, fires were lit, food was prepared, and a friendly and welcoming atmosphere befell the ten-wagon train.

After consuming another generous helping of dried meats, rice, beans, and hardened bread, I moved down the wagon train to find the other girls. I saw Beth in conversation with a similar-aged female. Caroline was chatting excitedly to a young man. I didn't find Martha until I reached the second-to-last wagon.

"Martha?" I whispered as I neared her, struck by the frozen way she was standing and staring. It was as if she had seen a ghost.

She didn't reply; she only stared.

I followed her eyes until I saw them: Jeremy, Agatha, and the short man, all seated with a group of others beside a fire behind the last wagon of the train. My heart began to pound loudly inside my chest. I felt weak and faint. I turned to Martha.

"Martha!" I said in a frantic whisper.

Martha slowly moved her eyes over mine.

"We have to get out of here," she finally whispered in return. "We can't let them see us."

"But where will we go?" I asked, keeping my eyes locked on the sight of our former captors, terrified they would look up and see me.

"Our wagon is miles back now. Our oxen have all been separated throughout this train. We have nowhere to go."

Martha turned her head to face the distant fire. In her eyes, I could see the reflection of the flames.

"Then we have to kill them," she said, her voice plain and loud, no longer a whisper.

I shook my head. "Martha, we can't—"

"I will do it," she concluded, turning to return to whatever wagon she had come from. I continued to stare at the fire. Agatha appeared thinner, even older. Jeremy looked down at his plate and fed in silence. The short man was involved in a spirited conversation with another of the wagon mates. They laughed and shouted in a nearly gleeful roar.

Slowly, I turned my back to them and slipped through the darkness to locate Caroline and Beth. Panic and fear now flowed through my veins, providing me energy I otherwise would not have had.

I found Caroline first; she was still chatting flirtatiously with the same young man I had seen her with earlier.

"I need to speak with you," I said urgently, motioning for her to join me at the side of the wagon. I could see in her eyes that she clearly sensed my fear, so she moved quickly to join me.

"They're here," I stated matter-of-factly. "Jeremy, Agatha, the short man . . . they are here."

I saw a wave of terror wash over Caroline's face. Her flirtatious smile fell into a pale, blank expression.

"Martha and I saw them at the back of the wagon train. They must have been rescued by these people. They didn't see us, but we certainly saw them."

"What are we going to do?" Caroline whispered, darting her eyes over my shoulder and toward the back of the train.

"Martha said she is going to kill them," I answered, following her eyes into the darkened distance.

"What?" Caroline replied. "She can't do that. Not with these people around. We have to—"

"We have to stop her," I finished her thought. "Let's find Beth, inform her of the news, and then together we will track down Martha. We have to find her before she does something that will get us all kicked off this train."

Caroline and I snaked through the wagons, keeping our eyes peeled for the two girls. We found Beth asleep on the ground near one of the fires. I left Caroline to wake her while I continued to search for Martha. I moved up and down the majority of the train three times before I finally located her. She was involved in a heated discussion with Jacob.

"They are our guns, and I want them," I heard Martha command.

"But the men will handle them now," Jacob replied, a calm smile on his handsome face. "You need not worry about danger now, miss. You are in very good hands with—"

"I want my guns!" Martha shouted, her shrill voice causing several fellow wagoners to stop what they were doing and stare.

"Martha," I whispered as I approached. "How about we find Beth and Caroline and sit near a fire?"

Martha snapped her head at me, a wild, fearful glaze gleaming from her eyes.

To my surprise, she obeyed, following me back toward the fire where Beth and Caroline were. Once together, we huddled away from other train members, careful not to allow any nearby ears to hear our whispered words.

"There is no way they can harm us now," I said softly to the girls, their faces just inches from mine. "There are far too many people here. There is no way they can do anything. We are best to just keep to ourselves, keep to the front of the train, and not mention the truth about them to anyone. Doing so may cause an issue."

"I want them dead," Martha stated. "I am not asking any of you to help me. I will do it myself."

"Martha!" Caroline squealed in a semi-whisper. "You can't do that. They will remove us from the train. You can't just shoot people and—"

"Those aren't people!" Martha retorted. "They are devils, and they deserve bullets in their skulls. I will handle it. You three just carry on about your usual business."

She stood from the huddled group and walked away. It was clear we would have to do far more if we hoped to subdue her murderous intent. As much as each girl shared Martha's fearful hatred of our former enslavers, coldly killing them now would certainly lead to our demise.

We had to do whatever we could to stop her.

Spotted

I KEPT A CLOSE EYE on Martha over the next few days. After the encounter with Jacob, Martha was moved closer to the front of the train. She didn't speak. She hardly even lifted her head. She simply marched along or sat still in place on a wagon bench or near one of the nighttime fires. Knowing Martha, it would only be a matter of time before she made her move.

I thought about revealing to Jacob the truth about who we were, including the three other refugees on the backside of his wagon train. I felt he wouldn't understand and would perhaps cast us—and them—from the train. The importance of our continued survival outweighed any need for truth and understanding.

From what I gathered, these *Saints* were deeply religious people. They may not have understood that our prostitution was never by choice, neither at the hands of our abductors or our self-managed encounters after we had broken free of them. There was one common fact that resonated through each and every choice and experience on this journey so far: survival. Each girl did what she had to do to continue living.

Beth and Caroline were also in wagons closer to the front of the train. As the days went by, we were given tasks to complete alongside the other wagoners. We did them with diligence and ease. Life on this train was far better than it ever had been on our previous train, both in captivity and after.

We girls huddled together by the fire each night, consuming our meals in silence. After seeing Jeremy, Agatha, and the short man at the back of the train, any feelings of comfort or serenity had diminished. Each girl struggled with her own personal hell of traumatic waiting. We knew it was only a matter of time before the dreaded trio discovered we were on the same wagon train as they were.

That moment came two days later. The train had stopped at a passing river. The water was wide and rumbling. Aside from the awesome Mississippi, this river was by far the most impressive waterway we had encountered on the trail thus far. I was standing near Jacob, filling several canisters with water, when I felt someone staring at me. I looked up to see Jeremy, standing just feet away, his face a mixture of shock and disbelief. I looked away, darting my eyes back to the river, but I knew I had been seen. I knew it was only a matter of time before he would approach me.

Later that night, as we four girls huddled near one of the many fires alongside the resting wagon train, Jeremy approached us. None of us spoke as we looked up at him in a unified, horrified stare.

"I'll be goddamned," he huffed, smirking. "Four of ya are here."

I could feel the rapid heartbeats of the girls next to me. My own heart pounded so loudly inside my chest that it nearly toppled me over.

Jeremy looked around, testing the scene for curious ears.

"Don't think I won't set things right," he hissed, lowering his head close enough that we could smell his breath. "This ain't over."

He disappeared into the darkness. None of us could finish our meals after that. We were far too sick with anxiety.

Martha spoke first.

"I will kill him tonight," she declared, more to herself than to any of us. "I will kill all three."

I didn't resist her words. None of us did. Each girl remained still near the fire, lost in the torment of her own mind.

Gunfire

I DIDN'T SLEEP THAT NIGHT. I lay awake for hours, listening to the constant sounds of the wagon train passengers. Coughing, moaning, snoring, speaking, you name it, it could be heard. The crickets of the nearby fields whirred and chirped in a unified chorus.

It was just before dawn when I heard the gunfire.

By the time I jumped out of the wagon I had been lying in, most of the wagon train had shuffled from their slumber. Men and women in various forms of dress scurried about in a confused haze. The gunfire had come from the back section of the train. I saw a shirtless Jacob rush past me with a rifle. Abraham and three other similarly aged boys followed suit, all with guns in hand. Within minutes, a female could be heard screaming, wailing. My mouth dropped open when I saw Martha, covered in blood, being dragged to the front of the train. I rushed to follow.

Several of the men moved to remove her blouse. It was clear she had been shot. Some of the women moved forward and started to assist. I stood by and witnessed one of the men fish a bullet from Martha's shoulder with a hunting knife. They packed the wound with what appeared to be cornmeal and sewed it shut. Martha continued to scream and wail the entire time.

Eventually, Jacob returned, still shirtless, covered in sweat and what I assumed was Martha's blood.

"It was one of the refugees," he declared to the group. "He thought this girl was an Injun, so he fired."

"No! No! No!" Martha bellowed. "He wanted to murder me! He wanted to kill me! He knew it was me!"

"Nonsense," a voice boomed over the crowd.

I turned to see Jeremy, who was also shirtless. Agatha and the short man were standing beside him. Agatha glared at me with a palpable rage that could be felt feet away. I assumed she too had been stitched and sewn up by the Saints when they had first rescued her and her fellow abandoned comrades. I imagined the bullet I had shot into her belly had been fished out and removed in the same fashion as Martha's. I was surprised the gunshot wound had not killed her, but I was certainly not in complete disbelief that she had survived after all. She was a brute force, as stubborn and strong as any ox.

"Liar! Liar! Liar!" Martha screamed, her voice a terrifying contrast to the silence of the fading night.

I moved toward her but was blocked by the women who were tending to Martha's injury.

"Stand back, dear," Jacob's mother instructed. "She is delirious. She needs space."

I felt Beth and Caroline creep up beside me. We turned as one, gifting a terrified stare at our three former captors. They stared back, Jeremy smirking, Agatha glaring, and the short man nodding.

It was only a matter of time before they got to all of us. One by one, we would be shot or somehow killed.

It was clear we had to get to them first.

Zechariah

B ETH, CAROLINE, AND I never left each other's side. Jacob had asked us to return to our assigned wagons but understood when we refused. He assumed we were just shaken due to Martha being shot, so he allowed us to remain together for the next several days. In that time, we managed a plan. One night soon, we would gather some guns and locate the three captors. There was no question that it had to be done. The longer we waited, the more likely we were to be killed. I assumed Martha had tried approaching them first, but I couldn't be certain. No one questioned Jeremy's story about assuming Martha's identity as a native. I knew it would be no different with us. One by one, they would find a way to pick each of us off and leave us dead along the trail. Any sense of security I once felt had long faded, even more so than it had the day when I had first seen that the three abductors were on the same train.

Martha remained inside the front wagon. I checked on her every few hours. She slept most of the time, but she was healing. Jacob said she would recover. Apparently, mistaken identity had been a common occurrence along the wagon train ride. Several had been either shot or shot at. Thankfully, no one had been fatally wounded, and the group had become quite proficient at fishing out rogue bullets and sewing up the wounds. Martha was a fortunate beneficiary of the suffering of others who had been mistakenly shot before her. The only difference was, Martha was not shot by accident.

That night, I told Beth and Caroline to meet me near the backside of the third wagon. I knew several shotguns were housed there. I had spent the last several days taking mental stock of each of the wagons. Nearly every occupant had some form of weapon, even the women. I had even seen some of the children touting pistols. It wouldn't be hard to locate some guns, but it would be challenging to take them unnoticed. I wasn't sure where our stockade of weapons had gone. Jacob had dispersed whatever was left of our single wagon throughout the rest of the train. One of the only things the wagon thieves had not made off with were our guns.

As per my instruction, Beth and Caroline were waiting for me behind the third wagon. It had been dark for hours, and from the sounds of the wagon train, most of the passengers were fast asleep.

As I had hoped, several shotguns were clearly visible from the backside of the wagon. The issue was the five sleeping occupants beside them. I reached inside and managed to grab one of the guns. Slowly and carefully, I pulled it from the wagon and handed it to Beth. Reaching back inside, I attempted to do the same with the second shotgun, but someone grabbed my wrist.

"What are you doing?" I heard a man's voice ask. My heart began to pound inside my throat.

A young man's face appeared, his hand still firmly gripping my wrist. He stared at me, and then at Beth and Caroline.

"We . . ." I started, but was cut short by the panic from within. "We thought we heard something out in the field."

The young man turned his head toward the open grounds surrounding the sleeping wagon train.

"I don't hear nothin'," he concluded, returning his eyes to mine.

"It was near the back of the train. We were gonna go investigate."

He squinted, the faint light of the overhead moon gleaming in his eyes.

"Let's get you back where you belong."

He slipped out of the wagon, his torso naked, his britches half buttoned, exposing the hair of his manliness. It had been some time since I had seen a naked man, much less a healthy and attractive one, so the image was unexpectedly arousing. He let go of my wrist and guided us back toward the front side of the wagon. Realizing his exposure, he lifted his pants and fastened the button.

"What's going on?" a voice whispered as we approached the front wagon.

Jacob appeared from the darkness, his eyes heavy with sleep.

"These girls heard something out behind the train," the young man replied. "I'm gonna go check it out. I wanted to get 'em back were they belonged first."

"Good man," Jacob replied, wiping his eyes with his shirt sleeve.

We watched as the young man disappeared into the night.

"That's Zechariah," Jacob announced. "He's one of my best men. He will take care of whatever is out there."

With that, Jacob motioned for us to return to our sleeping spots. We obeyed, although slumber never found us. I saw Beth and Caroline staring into the moonlight, the same as me. We had to do something, but God only knew how or when.

It had become an unspoken race of survival: the former captors versus their former slaves.

Martha's Return

THE NEXT SEVERAL DAYS passed by in the same repetitive fashion. The Saints were kind people. They were close and devoted. Each night, their campfire rituals were filled with singing and vibrant discussions of their faith. They were different than most of the religious people I had encountered while growing up in the cornfields of Missouri, or even during my time in the more diverse populous of St. Louis. I admired their devotion to their faith. Unlike so many on the trail, these people were only seeking asylum for their beliefs, a sense of belonging and community, and the freedom to practice their faith without rejection or political or social condemnation. They were not focused on gold nor personal wealth. What they were after was spiritual richness, not a dream of mining untold pounds of precious metal from the California earth.

I stayed close by Beth and Caroline. We took turns tending to Martha. She continued to sleep most of the time. The women who assisted her were very calm and knowledgeable in their way of providing care. It was clear that their time on the trail had garnered them a wealth of experience in this regard. They tended to Martha's wounds and ensured her daily intake of food and water. They were methodical and precise, never emotional nor uncertain.

I had become curious about Zechariah. Like Jacob and Abraham, he was young, handsome, and completely devoted to the well-being of the people on the train.

He was obedient to Jacob. It was clear that Jacob's family was in charge.

On the evening of the third night, I located Zechariah near one of the several campfires. I sat beside him and quietly consumed my portion of dried beef, rice, and beans. Zechariah didn't speak much to anyone. He consumed his meal and went about his business of checking over each of the wagons, ensuring their security, testing their wheels, and tightening any loose bits of canvas. For whatever reason, I was drawn to him. Perhaps it was his overall mystery and silence, or perhaps I was just so awfully bored that my brain craved something to focus on and wonder about. Jacob and Abraham were far more boisterous and open, so I didn't have to wonder much about their personalities. Zechariah's silence made him irresistibly alluring.

***

The days continued to roll into nights. We hadn't seen our captors since the night Martha was shot. They kept to themselves at the back of the train. Caroline had become the most worried of each of us.

"When are we going to try again?" she whispered to me as we settled into our fireside sleeping spots. "It's only a matter of time before they make their move on us."

The rolling days and my mental distraction over Zechariah had caused my anxiety regarding our former enslavers to ease some. For whatever reason, I no longer felt the urge to conspire an attack on them. With Zechariah's constant watchful eye over the train, I felt secure. I couldn't really explain it, so I didn't bother to try. I simply told Caroline that the time would come, and we would try again, but for now, we didn't need to cause any form of disturbance. At least, not until Martha was doing better.

****

A week later, Martha was able to stand and walk around. Her shoulder was healing very well, and she was no longer suffering the constant waves of excruciating pain she had felt since the night she was shot. For the first time in two weeks, she joined us at the fire.

"It was Jeremy," she stated plainly, keeping her eyes focused on the flickering flames. "He was awake. He saw me approach. He fired without even saying a word."

Beth, Caroline, and I listened intently.

"They will kill us. We need to kill them first," Martha concluded, her eyes never moving from the fire.

I lifted my gaze beyond the flames and saw Zechariah standing nearby. He had heard Martha. Her voice had been loud enough. She didn't try concealing her words.

He met my eyes, looked at Martha, and then returned his stare to me. He remained still for a moment before disappearing behind the closest wagon.

Later that night, once the train had settled into a nearly unified slumber, Zechariah approached me, startling me awake.

"What did that girl mean about killing people?" he questioned, his face just inches from my ear.

Groggy and confused, I lifted my head. I looked around; Beth and Caroline were fast asleep. I didn't see Martha. I assumed she was still taking advantage of her bed inside the wagon. It was only a matter of time before she would be deemed well enough to rejoin the daily marches and fireside sleeping.

"I'm not sure what you mean," I whispered back, slowly lifting my eyes to meet his gaze.

He stared at me for a moment, his handsome face illuminated by the dying embers of the nearby fire.

"I heard her. Plain as day. What's going on?"

I looked away nervously. Zechariah was intense and wise. There would be no fooling him with some pathetic lie or story, so I decided to just continue to deny what he was asking me.

"I don't know. I'm sorry," I said quietly. "Martha talks a lot. I think she is still affected by the gunshot. She's just talking crazy."

Zechariah continued to stare, moving his eyes over my face slowly and carefully. Finally, after what felt like an hour-long silent interrogation, he stood to his full height and disappeared into the nearby darkness.

I knew then that whatever we were going to do to our former captors had to be done as soon and as quickly as possible, or I would have to confess the truth to Zechariah.

I fell back to sleep undecided, never imagining I would never have a choice in the matter.

Living Nightmare

The next day was hard. The train moved through torrential rains. Lighting and thunder sizzled and cracked all around us. The trail was wide and open during the current trek. There were no trees nor any sort of covering. We were completely exposed and vulnerable to the elements.

As the train settled for the evening, everyone was worn and rain soaked from the storm-laden day. The usual campfire hymns and Bible verses were not sung nor spoken. There was an eerie silence over the entire train. The lack of the usual noises that accompanied the nights was startling yet somehow soothing.

I listened to the nearby crickets as I ate my dinner in peace. Martha, Beth, and Caroline were nearby. In a unified sense of obedience, we joined the overall silence of the train. I didn't hear another sound until the echo of blood-curdling screams and nonstop gunfire jolted me from a deep sleep.

By the time I realized what was happening, the wagon I had been sleeping next to was nowhere to be seen. In fact, the front two wagons were gone altogether, livestock and all.

I lifted my head and peered into the half-moon-lit distance. I scrambled to my feet as my vision focused on the sight of two dead women—parts of their faces missing—lying in the dirt just inches from me.

The gunfire continued. It cracked and echoed over the nearby prairie as fast and furiously as the thunderstorms that had pelted the train for most of the day.

I crawled toward the women, but it was clear there would be no helping them. Beyond them, I could see others. Countless others. Body after body littered the ground for as far as my eyes could see in the dim glow of the overhead moon.

I gasped as my eyes focused in on the sight of three children—all lying facedown in the dirt—the backs of their heads blasted open. My heart began to race as I crawled back to where I had been sleeping, desperate to find another living soul.

I turned toward where the other girls had been sleeping. I saw no one, only the blackened shadows of the open trail beyond. The missing wagons had left me open and exposed to endless miles of darkness. I crawled toward the nearest wagon, maneuvering my arms and legs over the fallen corpses of my wagon mates. I started to cry, but the emotion caught inside my chest. I had to stay focused. I had to be aware and alert. Whatever was happening was a living nightmare. Perhaps we were being attacked by another wagon train. I needed to remain levelheaded if I wanted a chance at survival.

As I neared the front wheel of the wagon, I saw Beth and Caroline, huddled together in a tight mass.

"What's happening?" I asked in a frantic whisper, causing their panicked faces to snap in my direction.

"It's them!" Caroline whispered. "They're killing everyone! They have Martha!"

I didn't need to ask more to understand what was taking place. Our former captors were ambushing the train, murdering their fellow wagoners as they slept peacefully on the ground.

The gunfire continued. It boomed and reverberated in a deafening roar.

"They each have more than one gun. They are shooting with both hands, just moving up and down the train," Beth chimed in, her voice strikingly less frantic than Caroline's. "They saw us. They saw you. But they only grabbed Martha and turned back, putting more bullets in those who they had already hit."

"They want us alive," I heard myself say, my voice high with pure tension and panic. "Where's Jacob? Zechariah? Surely they tried to stop them."

"They did. We saw them scrambling for their guns, but the three shooters moved precisely, as if they had been planning this. There was a struggle, but then the front wagons disappeared. I'm not sure what happened, but all three shooters are still alive. They moved back down the train without resistance, so Jacob and Zechariah are either dead or they fled."

"No," I heard myself continue. "They wouldn't flee. They wouldn't leave their people. This wagon train is their family, their kin. They would never leave them."

"I don't know," Beth said, shaking her head. "I don't know."

I watched tears stream down the young girl's face. Caroline only stared. The sense of shock and disbelief was so paralyzing and almost impossible to resist, but I did all I could to prevent it from taking hold of me. I would have to stay present and aware if I wanted to live.

All at once, the gunfire ceased. A deafening silence befell the train. There was no moaning, no screaming, no crying, only the constant chirp of the field crickets, their melody and song unaffected by the horror that had just occurred along the beaten dirt path of the California Trail.

In the quiet, we heard footsteps. Before we could move or react, Agatha appeared around the backside of the wagon we were huddled against, her face clearly lit by the half-moon.

I started to scoot backward, but she bolted forward, jumping into the air and landing her leather boots on my face. I struggled to scream as she began to beat me. I could hear her shouting in German as she pounded her fists into my face, blow after blow after blow. I started to see sparks of light as my consciousness seeped into blackness. I heard other voices, and the beating ceased. I couldn't see, but I could hear Jeremy and the short man yelling at Agatha, commanding her to stop.

"We need her!" I heard Jeremy shout. "I know you want your revenge, but you can't beat her senseless or kill her. Do it in other ways."

I heard Beth and Caroline screaming before their voices were cut short. I could still hear them moaning. I felt pairs of hands pulling at my arms and legs, binding them together. Tied like a wild boar, I was lifted and thrown into a wagon. I could hear Beth and Caroline nearby.

The voices of our captors faded into the distance before moving close again. The wagon we were in jolted forward, and the sound of the crickets was drowned out by the laughing and cheering of the three now murderers.

"We did it!" I heard the short man shout, his voice jubilant and excited like a child's.

Then, I faded into blackness.

The New Train

WHEN I FINALLY CAME to, I could sense sunlight around the wagon. The other girls were still sleeping. My eyes were swollen, nearly shut, but I could still clearly see the faces of those around me. I saw Beth and Caroline, both fast asleep. It was when my eyes roamed over Martha that I lost my breath. She was beaten so severely that I hardly recognized it was her. It took me a moment to realize I probably didn't look much better.

In the distance, I could hear the terrifyingly familiar voices. Per usual, I didn't hear Jeremy, only the short man and Agatha, their boastful banter more alive and vibrant than it had ever been months ago when they headed our former train.

It would be hours before we stopped. When we finally did, Agatha fetched us, pulling each girl to the edge of the wagon and untying her legs. We were guided to a nearby stream. Martha could hardly walk at all.

As we were led back to the wagon, I could see that the wagon train had been reduced to three. Each captor headed a wagon, the supplies within brimming so abundantly that the seams of the canvas coverings were pushed and stretched to their limits. The captors—now murderous thieves—had packed each wagon with as many supplies as they could possibly hold.

As before, we were a three-wagon train, with Martha, Beth, Caroline, and I again captives. But now, a devastating discard of thirty or more bodies had been left behind in the hours of distance between the present moment and the horror of the night before.

I caught Jeremy's quiet glare as Agatha led us back to the wagon. By herself, she retied our feet and tossed us inside. She was thinner than she had been weeks before, perhaps due to the trauma of her gunshot wound, which was now well-healed, but she was as strong as ever. No one spoke, but Martha groaned and mumbled as Agatha maneuvered her like a sack of cornmeal. Within minutes, the train was moving again, a repeated routine of once-a-day feedings and two water breaks comprising the twenty or so hours spent moving along the trail.

The men didn't start to appear until the evening of the fourth day.

As before, one wagon was emptied out each night, with a makeshift bed of straw and four flour sacks covered over with burlap placed in the center. I was the first to be with one of the men, a smelly figure who I could hardly see, both from the swelling of my eyes and the darkness of the wagon. He pleasured himself with my body for what felt like hours. It must have been an unreasonable amount of time, for I heard Jeremy shouting from behind the wagon for the man to hurry it along. I was with two men that night. Each girl was rotated more than once. It seemed like the captors were either trying to make up for lost time and income—both financially and in supplies—or they were cruelly trying to punish us for both escaping and attempted murder. My guess was the latter.

I thought about Jacob, Abraham, their parents, Zechariah, and the many faces, both male and female, young and old, of the wagon train we had spent so many weeks with. Had Jacob and Abraham not found us alongside the trail that day, we would have surely perished. Now, here we were, back where we started, sex slaves to a group of cold, callous creatures. They were more frightening now than ever. They had brutally massacred a wagon train of innocent devout men, women, and children. They too had been rescued by the Saints, yet they killed them all in cold blood with what appeared to be joyful abandon. Agatha and the short men regularly recounted the murders each night at the campfire. I could hear them as I lay in the wagon, their laughter and boasting of gunning down innocent lives both sickening and terrifying. As far as I was concerned, these people were evil, inhuman devils.

I wasn't sure if their murderous plan had been set from the start of them being rescued by the Saints or if the unexpected joining of their former slaves prompted their attack. Either way, it was done, and any hope of our escape and survival was completely diminished. Fate would have us die at the hands of these people, one way or another.

* * *

The nights blended. Man after man visited the wagon. We must have been trailing a populated train, for there was never a shortage of customers. I still could not see the men I was with, but none of the voices seemed to repeat. Every encounter felt new and fresh. There must have been enough virile and horny men to go around. From the rumblings of the captors, we weren't far from one of the several permanent camps and posts along the trail. I imagined that the sudden burst in vitality and arousal was due to the nearest train's rest, and rejuvenation of supplies from the nearest post. When the men were better fed and hydrated, they tended to be far more willing to take advantage of time with a female companion, even one who had no choice in the matter.

After what must have been a week since the massacre, Jeremy had Agatha and the short man drag us from the back of the lead wagon, untie us, and stand us in a line. My eyes were less swollen now, so I could see a bit better. My face still ached from the beating. Beth and Caroline hadn't spoken in days, and Martha still appeared bruised and blackened from her own run-in with the vicious captors.

"As before, you will walk from here on out. We don't have the chains. They was left behind in the old wagons. You know well there ain't nowhere to go. No place to hide. I think ya've seen now that we will always overpower you. Don't try to find any guns. You won't find 'em. They ain't as carelessly lyin' about this time. If one of ya gets outta line, you'll be shot, left to rot in the dirt like some dead rodent. Don't try nothin'. I promise I will shoot ya myself if ya do."

That was the most Jeremy had spoken to us since the beginning of our time together on the trail. Even during his sinisterly motivated courtship, he was never so vocal. The four girls remained still and quiet. No one spoke. No one resisted. We marched along behind the back wagon as we had done behind the previous wagon so many weeks and miles ago.

As the days continued to blend together, I began to wish the captors had murdered us as well. What fools we were to think these people wanted us dead. As soon as they saw us on the Saint's train, they knew what had to be done. We were their bread and butter—their key to survival. The fate of the Saints was sealed the day these three demons realized we had been rescued by the same train that had saved them from their own demise.

I grieved in silence for the selfless mistake those poor, innocent people had made.

Shocked

As before, we four girls huddled into a balled mass of flesh each night. Once our allotted time with the cycle of men had ended, we were left alone to sleep.

It was a clear night. The air was crisp and a bit chilly; the summer wind had calmed to a gentle whisper. I was the only girl awake; the others were sound asleep, each intertwined with the other. I heard voices. Sounds. I pulled myself from the pile, slowly and carefully, and tip-toed my way toward the muffled male voices. The moon was directly above us, now full, illuminating the wagon train with blue vibrant detail. I could see every shrub, weed, and dirt patch as my bare feet followed the ground toward the noises. It sounded like someone was being attacked. Perhaps one of the men from earlier had returned to rob the small three-wagon train. If so, I wanted to beg them to save the small group of enslaved girls. I was afraid they would make off with the wagons and livestock, leaving us vulnerable and alone on the wide-open trail.

To my complete shock, I saw Jeremy and the short man, both naked and hunched beside the third wagon. Jeremy was holding onto the side of the rear wheel while the short man thrust his bare pelvis against Jeremy's backside. Both men had their eyes closed, their faces gripped with what appeared to be a mixture of pain and pleasure. They moaned softly, both obviously attempting to conceal their lovemaking, but the clear air of the night had drifted the voice of their passion across the distance between the rear wagon and the pile of sleeping females. I stared for a few moments before trying to return to the other girls. Jeremy turned his head, his eyes only slightly open. As soon as he saw me, he stood straight, causing the short man to lose his balance. The short man fell to the ground, bare bottom first. Jeremy scrambled to find his trousers, stumbling over the pile of clothing that lay heaped beside them. In the pale moonlight, I could see their erections. The reality of their interaction was now clear and undeniable. I spun on my toes and bolted for the pile. I had barely made it back when Jeremy caught up to me, his still-bare torso glistening with perspiration, his belly and chest heaving as he struggled for air. He grabbed my hair and pulled me from the pile.

"Speak a word of this to the other girls and I will cut out your tongue," he hissed into my ear, his breath reeking of whiskey.

He threw me to the ground, finished fastening his trousers, and returned to fetch his shirt. In the slight distance, I could hear him scolding the short man. I lay still until the sun peeked over the horizon. I never attempted to move to rejoin the other girls. I was still stunned and shocked by what I had seen. I never knew that two men could make love. I had never thought about it nor had I even heard tell of it. It was clear Jeremy was embarrassed that I had witnessed the act. Still, as the sun rose and we were shuffled into our daily march, I never uttered a word of what I had seen to the others.

I knew very well that Jeremy would make good on his promise if I did.

Below the Surface

MY SHOCK AND EMOTIONLESS indifference over being recaptured soon fell into the always-open arms of anger. I silently began to rage. I raged for all who had died at the hands of these three people. The six girls we had lost over the months on the trail, the innocent lives of the Saints, and the recapturing of myself and the other three girls who had suffered long and hard to escape this forced life of agony and servitude all danced in an undying inferno along the forefront of my mind. I never said anything to the other girls, but quietly, alone in my private thoughts, I contemplated revenge. I no longer cared if my plans were sloppy or even realistic. I also didn't care if they would be successful. I just wanted to end this.

The days continued to morph into weeks. Finally, on a gray overcast afternoon, I made my move.

As Agatha led us to a powerful water source—a stream as fast and furious as I had ever seen—I gulped my share of water, dipping my face into the cold flow. When I lifted my head, I saw Martha, Beth, and Caroline doing the same. I moved back toward Agatha, who was looking upward toward the towering trees on the other side of the water. Without so much as a single moment's hesitation or thought, I pulled her bun with both hands, forcing the large woman to stumble backward. I pulled until I was waist-deep in the water. Agatha kicked and reached for her thigh-strapped pistol, but I dragged her beneath the current before she had a chance to retrieve it. I saw the other girls staring in disbelief. I held my breath and lowered my body underneath the surface, forcing the beast of a woman down to the muddy bottom below. In the clarity of the water above me, I could see the other three girls piling over Agatha. It was impossible for her to overpower the four of us. My lungs began to ache as I remained static under the water, my hands still firmly gripped around Agatha's still-tightly woven bun. There was splashing around us, and one by one, each girl was thrown from on top of Agatha. Jeremy and the short man were now in the water beside us, desperately tossing each girl out of the way in order to retrieve the drowning woman.

I was pulled up last, lifted and tossed into the air like a piece of discarded debris. Soaked and shivering, I crawled to join the other girls, who trembled together a few feet away.

We watched in a drenched silence as the two men pulled Agatha from below the rippling rush of the water. She heaved and gasped for air. A few more moments alone with her and we would have surely drowned her.

The men escorted her to the shore, watching over her as she coughed and panicked for air.

Without warning, she lifted her head and screamed something in German, her voice shrieking and high-pitched, before bulldozing toward us. She threw her body over the pile of soaking-wet girls. She flailed her arms and legs, punching and kicking at the frail bodies below her. The two men did nothing to stop her. They stood still and watched as Agatha sought her physical revenge.

Things were never the same after that afternoon. During the day, our hands were tied. At night, we were again bound like hogs. We were only untied when in service to the men. Afterward, we were dutifully retied and placed separately on the ground. We weren't allowed to speak nor touch. We were scattered far enough apart that any communication would have to be shouted or yelled, alerting our captors. They made sure of our complete disconnection from one another.

Agatha became more violent and cruel, especially toward me. One night, without any sound or warning, she dragged me by my hair around the campfire, shouting angry words in German. When she finally let go, she took chunks of my hair with her. I could see clumps of my dark-blonde locks gripped firmly in her fist. I reached up; my head was bleeding. My hair was soaked with the crimson fluid.

My anger and rage remained. If anything, it only heightened. I wasn't through with Agatha yet. She may have had the upper hand, but eventually, I would finish what I should have months ago when I shot one of her pistol's bullets into her body.

It was only a matter of time before I would kill her.

One by One

I WAS NEARLY ASLEEP WHEN I was jolted awake by a man's screaming. Hogtied and exhausted, I lifted my head from the dirt just as a man jumped from the backside of the bed wagon. Jeremy and the short man ran to meet him.

"That bitch bit me!" the man screamed, his voice high and panicked. He was gripping his groin; his trousers were still fallen around his ankles.

He reached for the pistol in the holster around his belt, but Jeremy stopped him. I watched as the frantic man was led away by Jeremy and the short man. His pain-driven bellowing went on for several more minutes before it finally faded. When Jeremy and the short man returned, they waited at the backside of the wagon as Agatha dragged Martha from within.

Martha's face was covered in the man's blood. It was clear she had bitten his manhood.

Jeremy and the short man held her down as Agatha took the backside of her pistol and began to knock Martha's teeth from her head—one by one.

Martha didn't scream. She barely flinched. She remained still as Agatha maimed her for life.

Once through, the captors retied Martha and tossed her into the shrubs beside the trail.

I never once heard Martha cry.

Back of the Head

IT WAS COMMON FOR us to go days without being fed. With the loot they had secured from the Saints, not to mention what was bartered and traded with the men who sought to spend time with us slave girls, the captors ate better than they had in months. Still, as before, we were provided a slop bucket with mashed cornmeal and bits of dried vegetables. Sometimes, there were bits of bacon or dried beef, and occasionally, the cornmeal was replaced with flour. But mostly, the gray, cold mush delivered the minimum sustenance needed to keep us alive. As before, we would pick and prod at the dirt during our few water breaks throughout the day. I found that digging for earthworms was quite easy. I began to enjoy the texture of their plump bodies as I maneuvered them around with my teeth. I found myself craving them during our long, silent marches. Often, I would opt to dig for earthworms rather than consume the mush we were given at random.

Several nights a week, long after the men had vanished for the night and Agatha could be heard snoring like a bear, I would hear Jeremy and the short man making love. They still attempted to keep their passion quiet, but I recognized the sound and listened quietly in the dark. Sometimes, I would see the other girls gazing silently at the starry sky. I imagined they too could hear the two men fornicating, but I wasn't sure if they comprehended what they were hearing. I never spoke of what I had seen. I didn't have a chance to. Agatha ensured our silence at all times. We were kept completely separated during the night. The captors would no longer risk another whispered plan of attack. We were left to our own devices. If one of us wanted to do something, we would have to follow Martha's lead and take matters into our own hands, or mouths, as in her case.

Martha consumed her share of mush along with the rest of us. The substance was soft enough for her to manage with her gums. Often, I would see blood dribbling from her mouth, but still, I never heard her cry. I wasn't sure if she was trying to remain unphased or stoic, or if the enormity of her pain was simply far too great for physical expression. The collective silence of the girls had become another being amongst the group. It was large and powerful. It spoke volumes in unheard words and phrases. I think we all could hear it: a mass of energy comprised of the collection of fallen souls who had succumbed to the terror of this wagon train.

✳

One evening, as I crouched over a hole I had dug for defecation, I managed to scoop the fallen contents and heave it with my still-tied hands at Agatha. It struck her in the back of the head. She reached and touched her hair, moving her hand to her nose. She shouted something in German before spinning around on her boots and charging at me. I held my breath as she beat and kicked me. I had become accustomed to Agatha's physical rage. She physically assaulted me far more than she did the other girls—payment for my two attempts on her life, I suppose.

Night after night, man after man, the shared existence of the girls had fused into one. We lived separately in a common hell, one that had no end in sight.

The River

The day we crossed the river was no different than any other. We had crossed waterways many times before, but this one was unique. It was deeper and far wider than any we had traversed previously. The oxen moaned as they were forced to enter the fast-moving current. I watched as the three wagons dipped below the surface, slowly inching toward the opposite shore. Agatha kept the girls back, waiting for the train to successfully reach the other side. One behind the other, each wagon lifted from the water and ascended the sandy bank.

Confident in the trail, Agatha led all four hand-tied girls into the raging water. I was in the middle; Caroline and Beth were ahead of me. Martha was behind me. Behind her was Agatha. Midway through the river, I lifted my feet and allowed the water to carry me away. I could hear Agatha shouting in German as the cold liquid rushed me away from her grasp. There was no way she would be able to catch me. I held my breath as the force of the water ushered me downstream.

When I finally lifted my head for air, I was stunned to see Martha beside me. She too had lifted her feet and joined me on the impromptu excursion down the river. For more than half an hour,

Martha and I bobbed along the current, allowing the dance of the river to swirl our submissive bodies with ease and grace. When the river finally slowed enough for us to fight against it, Martha and I trampled from the water and onto the shore without speaking. Both of us were extremely frail and weak. It didn't take much for the river to move us, and it would deplete every ounce of fading energy we had left to fight the stream, so we never tried. Only when the current began to ease and trickle did we attempt to exit the water.

Once on shore, Martha and I plopped onto the ground in shared silence. After several minutes of catching our breath, we began to laugh. I chuckled first, and Martha followed. For what felt like hours, Martha and I laughed until we were breathless again.

Eventually, I rolled over to her, wrapping my arms around her tiny body. She smiled at me, her grin wide and toothless. I pressed my face into her small bosom, which heaved from her laughter.

Without a sound of spoken communication, Martha and I began to weep. We were free. By God, we were finally free.

Miracle

THE FOREST WAS DARK and deep. Martha and I had been walking for hours. Several times, we stopped to feast on various berries and plant life. I dug for earthworms but found none. I helped Martha clean herself after she struggled to defecate. There were blood and some sort of bile. It smelled awful, but I cleaned her with care and ease.

We marched until the sun had well faded before finding a fallen tree to hide beneath. We slept soundly that night, no threat of forced sexual servitude or an unexpected beating threatening our existence.

When we awoke, we struggled to find edible plant life before marching on. There was no trail here. No beaten path forged diligently by the footsteps of thousands of migrants. Here, we forged our own trail.

Sometime around dusk, we heard gunshots. Terrified it might be our previous convoy, we huddled together in the brush and waited.

Dusk fell into night, but the gunfire continued. It ranged in distance. Finally, it ceased, but then we heard the voices. Male voices. Martha and I remained still and silent, hardly breathing as we listened in the dark.

One of the voices moved closer. It was only feet away. I could hear the words clearly.

"It had to have run this way," I heard a man shout.

The voice was familiar. I had heard this voice before, many times.

"Bring the sack!" the man shouted.

"Jacob!" I cried, lifting myself out of Martha's locked embrace and onto my feet. I could hear Martha gasping in the darkness. My sudden outburst must have taken her by complete surprise.

"Jacob!" I called again, trampling forward into the nearby brush. "Jacob, it's me, Meredith!"

Silence; only the sound of deafening night bugs remained.

"Meredith?" the man's voice finally replied.

I could hear someone rustling through the brush, moving toward the sound of my voice. I gasped when Jacob—to my complete and utter disbelief—broke from the thick brush and grabbed me in his arms. He squeezed me for a long moment, his breathing rapid and heavy.

"Martha is here, too," I whispered.

I could feel him sobbing, his tears soaking my hair.

Jacob didn't ask questions as he moved to fetch Martha, who crouched noiselessly in the nearby brush. Hand in hand, he led us from the forest and into a clearing. There, two wagons glowed orange from a nearby campfire. I could see Abraham and Zechariah standing nearby, their faces frozen and stunned.

"It's a miracle!" Jacob shouted, lifting Martha's and my arm with his hands. "It's a miracle!"

At Home

We rode along with the boys for three full days before they recounted the details of their escape the night of the massacre. As Beth and Caroline had told me, the boys had tried to defend their people, but the premeditated plan of the captors was too swift and steady for the boys' half-asleep fumble for their guns. Unable to stop the shooters, the boys pulled the front two wagons from the train, hoping the distance would give them the opportunity to gauge the full situation and resituate their counterattack. By the time they returned to the wagon train, the entire group had been massacred—brutally murdered. The captors had already taken us girls into the night, so the boys returned to the bloodied corpses of their family and loved ones.

They spent two days burying the bodies, providing each lost soul with a proper Mormon burial. They gathered up what supplies they could carry and loaded the two wagons they deemed most suitable for the continued journey. Fearing another encounter with the captors, they opted for a side trail that moved parallel to the main trail but was far enough away to remain concealed if need be.

Martha never spoke, but I recounted our struggle since the night of the killings. The boys listened quietly as I started from the beginning. I told them of our deception by Jeremy: the promise of marriage and a new life in the California gold mines. I detailed the months on the trail prior to our first escape from the captors. The boys listened silently as I relived the escape, the stay with the natives, and our dying last days before they had discovered us. The boys didn't flinch as I graphically detailed the weeks that had transpired since the last time we had seen them. Even the grotesque retelling of our numberless sexual encounters with an untold amount of nameless men didn't seem to faze them. Perhaps they were simply too shocked to react.

The boys wrapped us in blankets after feeding us the best they could. I could hear them sobbing separately at different times during the night. No words were needed to understand the enormity of their heartbreak. I could not imagine the trauma they faced having to bury their own parents, cousins, aunts, uncles, and lifelong family friends. Even though my own personal hell had deep merits when it came to suffering, my heart still broke for these boys.

The boys hunted, providing fresh meat for the camp. We feasted like royalty. I could not remember eating this well, even before my journey on the trail had begun. Martha managed to consume what she could, using her gums to soften and mash the shreds of tender meat, beans, and rice.

In a matter of days, both Martha and I looked and felt better than we had in weeks. We walked alongside the boys each day, helping to set up and break down camp each night and morning, assisting with the food preparations, and fetching whatever was needed when the boys skinned a fresh kill.

For the first time in months, I felt at peace. Safe. At home.

The Girls

THE BOYS NEVER SPOKE of revenge. Despite what the captors had done to their entire family, I never once heard any of them say one single word regarding serving due justice to the ones who had murdered their kin. I began to feel guilty about leaving Beth and Caroline behind. I could only imagine the extra helping of wrath they faced in Martha's and my absence.

Martha remained quiet. The once loud and defiant girl had shriveled into a pale shadow of the strong female she once was. I didn't speak to her often. She seemed to be content to be left alone most of the time, so I tried not to bother her.

Finally, on a cold night some two weeks after we had been discovered by the boys, Martha spoke to me in the night.

Her words were difficult to understand as her tongue flapped sloppily against her gums. I could tell she was self-conscious, so I made a deliberate effort not to appear strained nor confused by her broken speech.

"We need to go back for the girls," she managed to get out. "We can't leave them there."

I stared at her in the dim light of the nearby dying campfire. Around us, the boys had fallen asleep, their individual breathing and slight snoring a comforting ambience.

"We can't leave the boys," I whispered. "We will die out there on our own."

Martha shook her head.

"We go with them," she managed to say.

"Yes," I nodded. "We stay with them."

"No," Martha shook her head again. "We go with them to find the girls."

I stroked Martha's hair and held her until she fell asleep in my arms. She was right. We couldn't leave the girls alone with the captors. It wasn't fair. We had all suffered together since our first days on the trail. It wouldn't be right to leave them alone with them.

In the morning, I would speak with Jacob about the possibility of endeavoring to save my friends. I could only pray he would agree.

Tomorrow

I WAITED UNTIL MIDDAY BEFORE approaching Jacob with the idea to locate and rescue Beth and Caroline. He listened quietly as I walked alongside him, filling his ear with the idea to move our two-wagon train onto the main trail in hopes of tracking the captors.

Jacob never said a word. I felt a sense of hope from his silence. No words were better than a flat-out no.

That evening, as we all sat around the fire—the warm crackling of the flames the only sound in the dark—Jacob addressed the group.

"We will move onto the main trail tomorrow," he announced. "We will track the caravan that has the other girls. We'll do what we must to save them."

Abraham and Zechariah just stared at Jacob. Neither nodded nor said a word.

I felt myself sigh with relief. Next to me, Martha gripped my hand and squeezed it. We went to sleep that night in dreams of hope and prayer.

With the help of these boys, we—all four girls—could truly be free from the hell that bound us.

Your Sin

The next morning, we packed up the camp and moved the wagons forward through the nearby meadow. We turned the oxen north, marching them straight toward the nearby California Trail. It took about an hour or more, but finally, we broke through a line of trees with the worn and beaten trail clear in the distance.

We moved the wagons onto the path and started back west. The boys darted their eyes around us, listening for any sound of a nearby train. I could sense their nervousness. The last thing we wanted to do was stumble upon the captors unexpectedly. They had more than proven themselves lethal and unpredictable. Any sort of ambush would need to be carefully planned and executed. Failing to do so would more than likely result in our deaths, both the boys', mine, Martha's, and the remaining girls'.

We marched on in silence. The three boys were quiet as they each contemplated and conspired the hopeful encounter. The shared assumption was that the captors were well ahead of us on the trail. That night, it was decided we would continue to move without stopping. It was a quarter moon, and the sky was relatively clear. We had enough moonlight to move along the trail without the need for fiery torches, which would make us vulnerable and easy to see for miles. We couldn't take any chances. Keeping the oxen as quiet as possible was challenging enough as it was.

We traveled nonstop until the sun had long risen, blazing the rolling plain with its dry, heated yellow rays. We braked for water at a small creek and enjoyed a warm meal. The boys laughed and told stories of their kinfolk. They spoke of them as though they had not been brutally massacred. They spoke of them as though they would someday see them again.

Martha was quiet; per usual, she hardly uttered a word. She would mash what she could with her gums or would tear and press with her fingers what could not be managed by her mouth. She was vastly different than the girl who had once intimidated the rest of us girls and who had led the wagon train with confidence and focus once we had overtaken our captors. Now, she was frail, toothless, and almost mute. My heart ached for her. It was clear she truly did care for the girls, though. Had it not been for her insistence, we would not be on the trail after them now. I had not thought to go back for Caroline and Beth. I was far too wrapped up in my own survival. It was Martha who demanded we go back. It was Martha who was selfless enough to risk her life for them. It made me see her in a completely new light. Perhaps those weeks when she was in charge of the wagons had not showcased anger and cruelty, but a fierce and uncompromising love—a tough love hell-bent on keeping her girls alive.

***

Just before sundown, we could see a massive wagon train in the distance. It was the first major train I had seen with my own eyes. With our captors, we always kept a healthy distance just behind or just ahead of the nearest trains. This one was miles long. It snaked along the trail and over the hills as far as the eye could see. It was breathtaking to witness.

At sundown, the boys stopped the train and we set up camp. It was decided that there was no way the captors could be ahead of the train we had seen earlier in the day. It was far too big, and they would have had to have moved at record speed to be ahead of it. It was decided that they had to be behind us still, perhaps just a few miles or so, trailing the same train.

The boys also did not want to catch up to the train, for they knew it would be nearly impossible to break away once we had caught up and joined them. The trains were meant as a security and protection against the elements of the trail. There were safety and power in numbers. No responsible wagoners would allow a single party to join and then depart from an established and sizeable train. It was in our best interest, since our interest was that of a possibly violent rescue mission, to remain well behind the massive train that preceded us. More than likely, the convoy of murderous kidnappers and their two remaining captives would be along the way shortly.

The boys decided they would take turns on watch. If the captors were close enough, it was highly likely they would be working the girls. Therefore the short man would be passing by on one of the horses they had stolen from the Saints' fallen convoy on his way to conjure some male clients.

The anticipation of it all was far too energizing for me to even think about slumber. I tossed and turned in my sleeping spot, which was next to Martha near the softly smoldering campfire. Abraham and Jacob were asleep on the front side of the lead wagon, while Zechariah took the first hours of night watch, perched on the rear of the second wagon. Eventually, I moved to join him.

"Seen anything?" I whispered as I crawled through the wagon to sit beside him on the backside.

He turned to look at me, his expression slightly annoyed.

"Why are you up?" he asked, readjusting the rifle on his lap.

"Can't sleep," I answered, situating myself directly beside him.

"You should try to sleep. Tomorrow is another long day," he answered, keeping his eyes out over the blackness of the trail behind us.

"Zechariah," I started, moving my eyes from his face and into the distance beyond. "I've marched this trail exhausted, sick, dying . . . I've marched after hours of men slobbering and rolling on top of me. I've marched after vomiting all night, after lack of food or water for days."

I placed my hand on his knee.

"I think I can handle marching with a bit of a lack of sleep."

I could see him staring down at my hand in the darkness. I didn't mean to make him uncomfortable. It was just in my nature to be physically affectionate.

"God will forgive you for your transgressions," he muttered in the dark. "He will forgive you for your fornicating, but you must ask him and repent."

I sat stunned for a moment before pulling my hand away.

"Are you suggesting that I have fornicated by choice?" I asked, my voice now a bit louder than a whisper.

Zechariah didn't respond.

"Answer me, Zechariah," I commanded.

"It's your sin and your salvation," he stated plainly. "It doesn't matter what caused you to sin. You still sinned. Only you can repent for that."

Tears blinded my eyes as I stumbled through the dark wagon and out the front side. I located the blanket I shared with Martha and settled myself beneath it. How dare Zechariah assume that any of the encounters I had with the men were of my choice, my sin, or my transgression. How dare he free my enslavers of their forced servitude over my life and body. I would have never lain with any of the men I was with had I been given a choice. To fault me with the sin of fornication when my journey on the trail had begun in shackles and chains was infuriating.

I didn't speak to Zechariah again for days.

I Know You

After several more days of lightly trailing the massive wagon train ahead of us, it was decided that we would wait only one more night before moving to join the nearby train. The terrain was becoming more barren and dangerous. We also risked depleting our food and water resources by moving so slowly along the trail. We needed to either find the captors and rescue the girls or move to join the train. Another several days of lingering behind could mean running out of supplies before Deseret.

The boys were still focused on making it to Deseret. They had no interest in going to California to mine for gold. They wanted to join other Saints in the place of refuge their people had established some years prior. Of course, Martha and I had no choice in the matter. We were along for the ride no matter where the destination was. We were too far on the trail to try to turn back somehow, so our survival depended on the boys and where they wanted to go.

I lay awake that entire night, waiting and hoping to hear an approaching horse or wagon train. As with the other nights, though, the convoy of captors and captives never arrived. By the next afternoon, we had joined the nearby train.

The wagoners at the rear of the seemingly endless train were polite and welcoming. They made it clear they had no expendable resources to share but were more than happy to have us join the rear of the train. There was a relief in knowing so many travelers were ahead of us. The feeling of silent companionship was far more comforting than the deafening solitude of a two-wagon train.

I was disappointed that we never came across the captors and the girls. Martha didn't say a word.

That night, the boys socialized with the nearest wagons. We were welcome to join them, but Martha and I opted to stay near our own fire. I helped Martha mash her food and watched her eat in silence. I didn't have much of an appetite these days. I was both nervous about finding Caroline and Beth and still sickened and upset that Zechariah had shamed me for a sin I had no choice but to commit. I wondered if the other boys felt the same way. I assumed they did, so my interactions with them had become limited and brief.

* * *

It was at least a week or more since joining the train that Jacob noticed my silence and questioned me on it.

"Are you okay?" he asked as we marched alongside our first wagon, leading and keeping pace with the oxen. "You don't talk much anymore. Are you sad we didn't find your friends? We tried. I'm sorry we weren't successful."

"I know," I managed to squeak. "I appreciate the effort."

"How's your friend doing?" he continued, keeping his eyes on me. "She managing okay with her food? We can put some more water in her—"

"She's fine," I interrupted. "I make sure she gets enough."

From the corner of my eye, I saw him nod. He heeded the clear energy of my response and didn't attempt to pester me further. We walked for the rest of the day in silence, only the creaking of countless wagon wheels and the groaning of a multitude of livestock filling the space of sound around our ears.

Later that evening, I decided to venture up the train line. I smiled and nodded at my fellow wagoners as I passed their camps. Most ignored me, too worn and weary by the day's travels to really care about some stranger, but some eyed me curiously. Some returned my smile, but most just stared. I was about forty or so wagons ahead of my party when someone grabbed my arm.

"I know you," a voice whispered.

I spun around to face a dirty, groggy-looking man with a large, brown beard and missing teeth. He smiled at me and winked. "You's one of them whores out in the wagons. I fucked you about two months back. Remember?"

I was stunned. Of course, there was no way I could remember a single isolated encounter from months ago. Most of my time spent in the bed wagon had become one almost-forgotten blur of traumatic haze. I struggled to move out of the man's grasp.

"How 'bout we take another go at it?" he snickered, moving his free hand to his crotch and squeezing it.

I darted my head around, hoping to locate a witness to this frightening meeting, but found only disinterested backs and turned heads.

"Please," I managed to say in a shaking voice. "Please, I need to get back to my people."

"After we're through," the man grumbled, pulling me toward the nearby trees.

I started to scream, but he cupped his large, filthy hand over my mouth. I felt my feet stumble after him as he dragged us farther into the brush. The warm glow of the campfires was well behind us when he finally forced me to the ground and began to unfasten his trousers. I started to crawl away, but he kicked me from behind, the shock from his boot against my backside forcing me onto my stomach. I tried to scream again, but he pressed my face into the dirt of the small forest floor. I felt him position himself against my hips, the pulsation of his erect manhood sliding between the curves of my bottom. I felt him spit, the warmth of his saliva oozing over my skin and across my intimate regions as he located the orifice of his liking. I bit into the dirt in anticipation of his appendage's invasion of my body but was shocked when I felt him lift from behind me, completely gone as if he had levitated into the sky.

I heard a commotion. Some muffled shouting. Slowly, I dared myself to turn over on the ground. In the dim light between the trees, I saw two figures struggling for dominance. It didn't take long for one figure to overpower the other. I heard the slamming of fists over flesh. This went on for what felt like several minutes. When it finally stopped, I could hear the gurgled groans of the defeated. I managed to cover my exposed skin and attempted to crawl away, when a pair of hands pulled at my waist. I started to scream, this time my voice uninterrupted by any hands or dirt. The hands pulled me into the air and placed me on my feet. I couldn't see the face of the figure standing before me, but I recognized the voice immediately.

"Come," Zechariah whispered in his calm, still tone. "Follow me."

He held my hand as he led me through the darkness of bushes and trees. Within several minutes, we broke from the brush and appeared alongside the rear two wagons of the train—our wagons. Abraham and Jacob were asleep on the ground; Martha was nearby, wrapped in a blanket beside the still-burning fire. Zechariah dropped my hand and moved to fetch a spare blanket. He returned, wrapped it around my body, and led me to the fireside. He disappeared again, returning moments later with a tin cup full of water. I consumed the liquid and closed my eyes. The shock of what had just occurred was starting to wear off, and I was suddenly experiencing my fear and anger.

Zechariah sat beside me as I started to weep. He wrapped his arms around me and pulled me close to his chest.

It was there I remained for the rest of the night.

The Baby

WHEN I AWOKE, I was next to Martha. The smell of fresh flap-jacks and coffee filled the air. Per routine, I stood, readjusted my clothing, splashed my face with cold water, and joined the order of wagons as the day's march commenced.

Zechariah kept his distance. Although I never really tried, he never allowed me the chance to thank him for rescuing me the night before. Only when the train settled in that evening was I able to find him alone.

"Thank you, Zechariah," I said firmly, my voice shaking but my words weighted with sincere truth. "Thank you for what you did last night."

Zechariah didn't turn around. He was busy tending to a tear in the canvas covering of the back wagon.

"How did you know where I was?" I asked, keeping my eyes locked on the back of his head. "Were you following me?"

"You should get you something to eat," he suggested, never lifting his eyes from the work of his hands.

"I will," I replied, slightly annoyed. "Were you following me last night?"

After another minute or two of fidgeting with the canvas, Zechariah turned to face me.

"Go eat," he commanded, locking his eyes on mine.

I felt my heart flutter as his watery stare positioned itself over my eyes. Despite his aloofness and cold demeanor, I was still very drawn to him. The mystery of Zechariah still tempted my curiosity and electrified my veins.

He didn't wait for a reply. He disappeared behind the wagon and into the darkness of the empty trail beyond. I joined the fireside meal and consumed my lot in silence.

***

It was the screaming that woke me. The wailing. Several men were shuffling from their campfire beds as I managed to my feet. A few wagons up from our own, a woman could be heard shrieking into the night.

There were very few women on the trail. The Saints had been an exception. Most of the gold mine-bound trains were comprised primarily of men. They were either young bachelors or married men who had left their wives at home to tend to the children, farms, or businesses, with the plan to return rich or send for them once a fortune had been dug from the ground. In some rare cases, the women joined on the initial migration.

A few moments later, the boys reappeared, eager to reload their rifles and shotguns.

"What's going on?" I asked Jacob, who shuffled through the front of the rear wagon for the artillery case. "Why is that woman screaming?"

Jacob remained silent, focused on his search for the case.

"Found it," I heard Abraham say from beside Jacob.

Together, the two men loaded their weapons and returned to the commotion.

"What's the matter?" I asked one of the men in the wagon ahead of our own. He was busy resituating himself beside his campfire, intent on returning to sleep.

"Sir?" I asked again.

"Her baby," the man replied, never looking up from his fireside bed. "Coyotes got 'em."

My heart dropped at the visualization of what the man had just revealed. I didn't know there was a baby nearby. I had never heard it cry nor coo. I returned to the campfire stunned and disturbed.

"What's going on?" Martha mumbled once I returned beside her under our shared blanket.

"Coyotes took someone's baby," I answered, my eyes welling with tears. Martha wrapped her arm around my shoulders. We fell asleep in a shared restless slumber.

South Pass

THE SEARCH PARTY NEVER found the baby, nor did they find the coyotes who took it. The wagon train moved on the next morning. The woman screamed and wailed for hours. The sun had long set when she finally depleted her voice of sound.

The incident haunted me for days. My heart broke for the poor mother. A part of me wanted to locate her and try to comfort her, but I knew it was best for me to stay with my own wagon. The woman wept every night. A week after the disappearance of her infant, I had grown accustomed to the sound of her wailing. Then, one night, her crying ceased altogether. I never heard her make another sound. The man from the wagon in front of us later told me that the mother had died a few days prior. She was buried, like so many others, alongside the rugged, worn pathway of the trail. They said she had shown no signs of illness. It was assumed she simply died of an overly broken heart.

* * *

The summer was slowly inching into autumn. The nights were colder and the landscape drier and more desolate. The wavy grass plains we had ventured through for months were slowly becoming vast desert beds and towering clay-like mountains. Trees had become fewer in number, so the sun pelted us with its relentless heat and shine for most of the day.

The boys had begun to chatter about our eventual break with the train. From the information they had gathered, this train was taking one of four splits in the trail that would take them directly to the California gold mines. The boys wanted to veer to the southernmost trail, the one that would take us into northern Deseret. One of the men from a wagon much further up the wagon train promised he would notify the boys the night before the train would come to the bypass. He promised that the back half of the train would stall for a few minutes to ensure our safety onto the alternate trail. I started to worry about that day. I had grown used to the mass of wagons ahead of us, so many wagons that I could never see the front of the train, even when the convoy turned and wove along the winding trail. To suddenly lose that sense of community would be frightening, despite the many months I had spent in just three- or two-wagon trains.

There was a mention of a place called South Pass, and the boys started to plan our departure. Sometime around midday the following day, the wagons ahead of us halted, and we pulled our two wagons from behind them and onto a southern turn. I sat on the backside of our rear wagon, staring as the few stalled wagons watched us trek along our new path for a bit before eventually moving forward to rejoin the rest of their massive convoy. The feeling of the missing companions—most of whom I had never met, even those in the wagons closest to our own—was immense and striking. Our two wagons trouped along the turn in the trail. Our destination was now just a few weeks away.

Despite the sudden isolation, I felt I had left a part of myself on the trail before the split—the part of me that had endured so many months of pain and torture, so many hours spent in forced service to the fleshy needs of innumerable nameless, faceless men. I felt a sort of rebirth as our two-wagon train marched toward Deseret and a place the boys called Great Salt Lake City.

Within the month, we would make that our home.

Great Salt Lake City

THE DAY BEFORE WE made it to Great Salt Lake City, we saw several natives observing us in the distance. No one said it, but the fear and anxiety over what might happen haunted our travels for the entire day. We were vulnerable on our own, and tales of savage and often-violent natives continued to dominate fireside conversations, especially amongst our former train.

There was a sense of relief as we pulled into Great Salt Lake City, not just because we had managed to avoid a feared ambush by the natives, but also because we had finally made it to some form of civilization. The bustling town was the first permanent living establishment I had seen since leaving St. Louis. Just a few years old, the city was maturing quickly due to the constant flow of westward-bound gold-seekers who opted to reload and restock in the city. This allowed for Great Salt Lake City not only to secure the goods they needed from the civilized east, but also to accumulate the means necessary for a new city to flourish.

Great Salt Lake City was a refuge for the Saints, a people often marginalized and persecuted, even by the United States government. Like the boys' family and friends on the tragically massacred train, the Saints here were warm and welcoming. We were fed, given new clothing, and housed in rooms with actual beds. It was the first time in months where I felt like an actual civilized human being and not some indentured animal-like slave, forced to rummage through the dirt for food or left to exist in my own filth for weeks on end. Here, I felt like a lady again. At least, as close to a lady as I had ever been.

The boys did not disclose that Martha and I were not Saints ourselves. We attended church services alongside them as though we were as familiar with the teachings of Joseph Smith and the holy scriptures as they were. I was given my own copy of the Book of Mormon, and Martha, who was semi-formally educated, began teaching me to read.

Martha was shy and quiet around the others. She was self-conscious about her missing teeth. She hardly spoke and would never smile. Only with me, in private, would she say a few words and even laugh as I recounted funny stories and memories from our time on the trail together. Despite the absolute living hell of most of our journey, especially during our time with our captors, there were fond moments to be remembered and cherished, mostly surrounding the sisterhood of the girls, the time spent with the Saints, and even the feeling of freedom and hope that had surrounded the Martha-led escape from those who had enslaved us. Martha and I never stopped talking about Beth and Caroline. We would often make up stories of how they had overpowered Jeremy, Agatha, and the short man and were now headed west without them. Martha came up with a version that had them as outlaws—robbing the nearby trains of supplies and loot, a fearsome reputation accenting their journey—so much so that the government had sent the army after them.

It was comforting to imagine that our two friends were not only surviving, but thriving. Deep in my heart, though, I felt that their servitude and suffering were only continuing. Who knew where the captors had them today? It was possible they had made it to San Francisco, but it was also possible they were still moving along the trail, serving the nearby wagon trains with purchased female accompaniment.

Each night, just before I fell asleep in the bed I shared with Martha, I said a prayer for our two friends, asking God to keep watch over them, to keep them safe and alive, and to somehow guide them to freedom.

Winter

THE BOYS TOOK JOBS as farmers. We didn't see them much anymore. The farm they managed bordered the outskirts of the small city. Martha and I worked for the food and board we were given by assisting the family we lived with, a family of six—a married couple and their four children. We aided the wife with household chores and various church service duties. Everything these people did revolved around their involvement with the church. The entire city was a church parishioner. No one failed to show up for services unless they were deathly ill or caring for someone who was. Everything was dropped when church commenced. I admired the passion and devotion these people shared for their understanding of love and God.

A few weeks after we had arrived, I was offered a job as a seamstress. I had only vague knowledge of sewing; I had patched a few quilts and torn trousers during my affirmative years on the various farms and households I grew up in, but I was certainly no master with a needle and thread. An older woman called *Mother* offered me the position. I didn't know what her actual name was; everyone simply referred to her as Mother. She was widowed, her seven grown children married and residents of the city. She worked from her small two-bedroom home, where she employed five other girls. We were paid a meager wage, but it was enough to allow us to contribute to the burgeoning commerce of the town.

The wagon trains moved through in great numbers. The Salt Lake Cutoff had grown in popularity with gold-hopeful migrants, especially since the diversion allowed for trade and goods replenishment, with the return to the main trail just a few short miles longer than had the stop been bypassed. The Saints were glad to trade with the travelers. It was the key to their survival. Great Salt Lake City was isolated from the rest of the nation. Without the passing wagon trains, the Saints would have surely perished. Their petition for statehood had been sent to Washington, DC. It was the hope of the church for their small but effective self-contained government to be recognized by the nation and their statehood granted. The final word had yet to come, although the latest news had confirmed that Congress was involved in the matter.

Martha remained at home most days. She headed the household chores and duties alongside Mrs. Bethel, the wife of the family we stayed with. To Martha's and my great shock, many of the men here had more than one wife. This was foreign and confusing to us, and apparently much of the reason why most of the country and even the government were opposed to these people. Mrs. Bethel was Mr. Bethel's only wife, but we encountered many families where there were two, even three wives per one man. The entire concept baffled me, but over the course of several weeks, I became accustomed to it.

***

The days continued to weave into weeks, and the weeks into months. Soon, the air chilled and the wagon trains ceased. Any trains still out on the trail risked becoming snowbound, a tragedy that had befallen a group called the Donner-Reed Party. They had forged a new path on the trail some years prior, causing their delay and entrapment in the Sierra-Nevada Mountains. Their demise was a common story told fireside on many wagon trains. The truth, which was far darker than most fiction, had them resorting to cannibalism just to survive. Their mistakes and resulting misfortune were the oft-repeated warning that kept most trains far ahead of the winter months.

The ground began to harden; the crops were tilled, and snow now blanketed the small city. Growing up in Missouri, I was familiar with winter. Martha, who had grown up in various places across the American South, had a harder time adjusting to the frigid temperatures. Some days, the snow and cold were too great for me to venture the two-mile walk to Mother's, so I would remain home with the Bethels, assisting in whatever household chores could be managed without the need of venturing outdoors. The Bethel children—three girls and a boy—were all similar in age. They were very well-behaved and hardly spoke unless spoken to by the adults. They kept to themselves and only displayed the playful, boisterous behavior of children when allotted free time to play and explore outdoors. During the winter, though, they remained indoors, silent and studious to their homeschooling and religious studies. The children could quote scriptures from both the Bible and the Book of Mormon with perfection. I was amazed at how knowledgeable and wise they were to their family's beliefs. It was inspiring, albeit a bit unnerving.

Mr. Bethel conducted church services in the living room when the weather prevented us from making it to the city's meetinghouse. Martha and I would sit quietly as Mr. Bethel read from the holy scriptures and prayed for the family's health and well-being. This was only the second Deseret winter for the Bethels. They had only just arrived in Great Salt Lake City a year and a half prior.

***

The winter dragged on, and my boredom became nearly unbearable. Martha would always remain indoors, but I would often venture outside, usually the backyard, just to breathe the fresh winter air and enjoy a bit of solitude from the crowded confines of the Bethel home. It was during my outdoor meditations that I would think about Emma, hoping she was healthy and well with the natives. I would think about Beth and Caroline, hoping they were safe from the trail now that winter had taken over. I even wondered about Jacob, Zechariah, and Abraham. It had been several weeks since I had seen them at church. My heart still skipped a beat whenever my eyes saw Zechariah in the flesh. The physical labor of the farm and his heartier diet had resulted in his body becoming larger, stronger, and more impressive. One night, once I was sure Martha was asleep, I pleasured myself to the thoughts of Zechariah. I imagined him making love to me. Unlike my experiences with the nameless, faceless men on the trail, my fantasy of Zechariah was less about sex and far more about intimacy. I craved his touch, his voice, and the feeling of his body close to mine. I assumed he would soon marry, perhaps building a farm of his own. I couldn't imagine that the three young, handsome bachelors would remain together on the farm much longer. As good Mormon men, it was their God-instructed duty to marry and be fruitful. Most Saint homes had at least five or more children. Vast reproduction was as much a central part of their culture as their belief in the teachings of Joseph Smith.

***

As the winter slowly eased into a milder state, the year now 1851, I was again able to return to work at Mother's. I relished the labor. Anything besides being cooped up in a small house of eight was a paradise.

That Sunday, the family would return to church, the first time back in weeks for many neighboring families. Only the families who lived closest to the meetinghouse were able to continue to attend without interruption. Everyone else practiced the services within their own homes, a duty always headed and performed by the man of the house.

I saw Zechariah and his brothers sitting in the back pew of the large sanctuary. As the service ended and the parishioners marched down the aisle and through the front doors of the temple, I caught up with Zechariah.

"Hello, Zechariah," I said meekly, my voice barely louder than a whisper. "How've you been?"

"Fine," he replied flatly, a tinge of disinterest in his voice. "How are you?"

"Good," I answered, keeping my eyes focused on the ground before us. "The Bethels are nice. I'm working with Mother as a seamstress. Now that the winter is calming down, I've returned to work. I'm so grateful because it was really starting to get to—"

"I have to go," he interrupted.

"Oh," I said in a half whisper. "Okay. See you soon, then."

He didn't reply. I watched as he moved to meet up with his brothers, who were waiting in a canvas-less wagon. The other boys nodded at me as Zechariah climbed aboard. I watched them disappear from sight before managing to move my feet toward the Bethel home. A sense of annoyance draped over me as I made the two-mile journey alone. It frustrated me that I was so interested in Zechariah, yet he seemed to have absolutely no awareness of me. I thought back to when he had shamed me for my days spent as a forced prostitute. A small flame of rage reignited inside me at the memory of his words. That helped to ease the cold chill of his ignorance and appease my need to dwell on him.

I returned home and joined Mrs. Bethel and Martha in the kitchen. We prepared Sunday supper, set the table, and joined the rest of the family for the traditional after-services meal. As I listened to the sounds of the family chattering and laughing amongst themselves, I silently vowed to myself that I would no longer think nor care about Zechariah.

I would treat him with the same disinterest and near disdain as he treated me.

Martha Marries

MARTHA HAD A SUITOR. A young man named Benjamin Redding had taken a liking to her. Naturally, they met at the meetinghouse, the only social activity Martha ever took part in. He started showing up at the Bethels with flowers and small handmade gifts. Of course, Martha was smitten, but also plagued by her overwhelming self-consciousness.

"I don't know why he likes me," she lamented one night as we lay side by side under our pile of home-sewn quilts. "I'm not pretty like the other girls. I don't have my own teeth."

"But he likes you, Martha," I answered, gripping her hand underneath the blankets. "He wouldn't keep stopping by with gifts and flowers if he didn't."

"I just don't know," Martha continued, a long sigh trailing her words of concern. "Once he finds out about my past . . . about who I've been and what I've done, he won't be interested any longer. That I know for certain."

"No, Martha," I whispered. "If he truly likes you, he will understand all that. We didn't sell our bodies by choice. We were slaves. We had no choice. A smart, understanding man will see that. If anything, he might take pity on you. Not judgment."

Martha's worry over the matter was settled a few days later. She had agreed to join Benjamin on a several-mile walk to his family farm. Along the way, she told him of her time on the trail and of her forced sexual servitude. She cried as she later recounted the conversation with me alone in our shared bed. She was overwhelmed by his understanding. Unlike Zechariah, Benjamin told her the sin was that of the captors, not hers. Benjamin said God would forgive her and punish those who had wronged her spirit, soul, and flesh. Martha was completely overcome by this grand honesty and understanding. As happy as I was for her, I couldn't help but feel a slight tinge of jealousy that Zechariah had not been able to grant me the same acceptance and forgiveness. Where Benjamin absolved Martha of her cumbersome burden with just a few loving words, Zechariah condemned me with his. Despite my vow, I was still having trouble not thinking about Zechariah. When I had gone a solid day without wondering what he was doing at that very moment, my brain made up for the oversight by filling my dreams with his voice and image—dreams that ranged from animalistic sex and passion to simple images of us holding hands, raising children, and even as an old couple. I would be particularly foul in mood the mornings after I had dreamt of Zechariah. Martha learned not to pester me much when she sensed my need for silence.

As the winter continued to ease into early spring, and early spring into mid-spring, the first wagon trains began to appear. A silent part of me felt tempted to join one of them. The quiet and monotony of daily life here with the Saints were starting to become overwhelming. Although my previous journey on the trail had been traumatic, it was at least an onward-moving adventure of sorts. Here, in Great Salt Lake City, one day blended into the next with colorless memory and uneventful drab. I missed the excitement of traveling, despite the obvious hardships.

***

A month later, Benjamin asked Martha to be his bride. At the Bethel dinner table, she cried as she recounted his proposal. I was truly overjoyed for my friend, but a deep part of me could not help but feel just a slight bit envious. The dark emotion restoked the flames of my rage toward Zechariah.

A few weeks later, Martha was gone—married. She moved with Benjamin to the small farm he had built with his father and brothers. It wasn't far from his family farm, so Martha spent much of her time tending to her own home's housework or assisting her new mother and sisters-in-law with theirs.

Eventually, Martha stopped visiting the Bethel household altogether, and I only saw her during church services at the meetinghouse. Without Martha in the home, the Bethel's farm became an unbearable prison of monotony and boredom. I craved an escape. Anything. Just something to ease my mind of the relentless parade of nothing that compiled the hours of my days.

To my surprise, that thing would come far sooner than I ever could have expected it to.

Paul Benson

PAUL BENSON WAS A tall man, raised up on the shores of Carolina. He was strikingly handsome, with sandy-blond hair and sea-green eyes. I was instantly drawn to him. A young bachelor with gold-dust dreams filling his eyes, he was a part of one of the early-season wagon trains.

He appeared at Mother's one day, sent by his party with a pile of torn and tattered clothing for us to repair. Mother accepted the order and began divvying out the garments to her herd of seamstresses. I couldn't help but stare at Paul, who seemed to have a similar issue keeping his eyes off me. I was surprised to see him waiting outside Mother's after my workday had ended and I started my walk back to the Bethelses'.

"Howdy," he said with a warm smile. "My name's Paul."

At first, my responses to him were brief and limited at best, but after a while, I began to warm to his vibrant, smooth Southern charm. His personality was as attractive as the rest of him.

Mrs. Bethel eyed him suspiciously as Paul dropped me off at the front gate of the large wooden fence that surrounded the Bethel homestead.

He bowed and tipped his hat, filling my ears with words of promise concerning his return to see me later that evening.

"Best to watch out for the traveling kind," Mrs. Bethel warned as I settled myself in the kitchen. "They are only passing through, so it is best to just keep things strictly about business and nothing more."

I felt her eyes on me as I sifted through some of the raw vegetables that had been left for me to slice, chop, and dice. I didn't say a word. I didn't want to ruin the unexpected attention Paul had shown me. It had been months since a man had fancied me, one of the wagon patrons or otherwise.

As promised, Paul returned that evening with a large bunch of handpicked wildflowers in his fist. I blushed as I took them from him, the feeling of his hand against mine sending an electrified pulse throughout my entire being.

We walked along the beaten trail toward the center of Great Salt Lake City. Paul filled the air with stories of his time on the trail, grand tales of overcoming native attacks and even overpowering cholera. Of course, based on my own experience on the trail, I didn't believe either story, but I humored him with a listening ear and constant smile.

As we neared the center of town, Paul gripped my hand.

"I know this is sudden, but would ya be willin' to join me to California?" he asked, more in a stumbled blurt than a well-prepared proposal.

I stared back at him, shocked by his words, yet somehow calm and collected.

"There is something about me you need to know," I started, my voice calm and free of the nervousness that I assumed would be plaguing it right about now. "I'm not here by choice. I was captured and used as a sex slave for months. I was rescued by a group of Saints, who brought me here. I'm not a Mormon girl, just an orphan from

Missouri. I'm not a clean girl, Paul. I'm sure I'm not the type of girl you'd be interested in taking with you to California."

Paul just stared back at me, his mouth slightly agape.

Finally, he shook his head and laughed.

"Nah, I don't care about all that," he said in his singsong way. "We all have our trials and tribulations. God got ya through it, and here ya are. I just can't help but like ya, Miss Meredith. There's somethin' in your eyes I ain't never seen in any other female. Some kind of fire and beauty. It's exciting and wonderful. I just want to be a part of it."

I was stunned—bewildered.

"You mean, you don't care that I've been with dozens of men? More than I can even count?"

He smiled and shook his head.

"Nope. Don't. Not a bit."

I just continued to stare, more out of disbelief than anything else.

"I don't know, Paul. I mean, I certainly appreciate your honesty and your ability to see beyond my past, however forced it may have been on me, but I am secure here with the Bethels. They treat me right. They feed me well. I'm not sure if I want to chance my life again by moving out over the rest of the trail. It's just—"

Paul pulled me into his arms, pressing his lips against mine. A sizzling, zapping sensation radiated throughout my body. I felt myself go limp in his grasp, the feeling of his wet lips against mine igniting the sensation of my womanhood. I could feel his pulsating erection pressed against me. Flashes of countless encounters with strange men danced across my memory, forcing me to break from the embrace.

"I best be getting back to the Bethelses'," I whispered, wiping my mouth of Paul's wet kiss. "Thank you for this walk, Paul. I greatly appreciate your kindness."

"Isn't there anything I can do to convince you?" Paul begged as I started to walk away. "You could help me mine the fields if ya wanted. We could buy a house. Have babies. Grow old together."

"I've only just met you, Paul!" I exclaimed. "Today! I only just met you today!"

"But don't ya feel it?" Paul asked, dashing closer. "Don't ya feel the same fire I do? My body aches just standing close to you."

I darted my eyes back and forth over his. I couldn't make out if he was just impulsive, stupid, or plain-out crazy.

"Goodnight, Paul," I said, swiftly turning on my heels and floating away.

I could feel him staring at me as I disappeared into the darkening evening. I made it home and went straight to bed, bypassing the family's evening Bible study.

That night, I was awakened by the same trail of dreams regarding Zechariah. Sex, marriage, children, and old age—I saw it all, over and over—in a flashing rainstorm of fantastical folly.

The next morning, I left an hour early for Mother's. I needed to find Paul. I knew his wagon train was set to depart before noon.

"All right," I said as I approached him from behind. He was standing near one of his mules, pulling what appeared to be ticks off its backside. "I will join you, but no promises of marriage, or babies, or anything crazy like that. I just need to leave here. I need something more, so I will join you."

Paul smiled and grabbed me by the waist, lifting me from the ground and spinning our conjoined bodies in a celebratory twirl.

"Go home and get your things," he said after he lowered me back to the ground. "We leave in an hour."

Back on the Trail

Mrs. bethel remained silent, but Mr. Bethel and the children all wished me well as I packed my few belongings, hugged and kissed them goodbye, and walked off their property for the very last time.

I wasn't sad. I wasn't remorseful. I was simply grateful for their kindness and hospitality. I was mostly relieved and excited just to be out of there.

Paul smiled as I approached. I was introduced to several of his fellow wagon mates. This train was small, only about a dozen or so wagons. They had departed far earlier than most of the other trains would have. Most were only just now embarking on their journeys, careful to allow enough springtime to grow the grass needed for their livestock to feed on along the trail. This train had decided to take their chances by heading out weeks earlier than the rest, a risk that had paid off. Despite Paul's tall tales of aggressive natives and overcoming cholera, this wagon train appeared to be in fine shape, especially considering the length of their journey. Most wagoners looked rail thin, gaunt, and starving by the time they managed to pull their wagons into Great Salt Lake City. This train had been well prepared for the journey thus far.

Without any pomp or circumstance, the wagon train departed Great Salt Lake City and headed for the Salt Lake Cutoff. In less than two hundred miles, we would be back on the California Trail.

I walked beside Paul, who chatted incessantly. His words filled the air and were a needed comfort and warmth. I never tired of the sound of his voice, even when the sun had begun to set and the train settled in for the night. Paul not only chatted abundantly to me, but also to everyone in earshot. He spoke of his big dreams of what he intended to accomplish once we reached the California gold mines. He spoke of his future, his past, and everything and anything in between. He spoke of his kinfolk, his boyhood dog, even his first girlfriend. The only time he was quiet was when he was asleep. He even continued to speak nonstop while eating. It was charming and amusing to witness. Before I had met Paul, Emma was the only person who I knew who could speak without pausing. Paul could speak circles around Emma though.

I fell asleep that night beside Paul and a dying campfire. I thought of Emma, hoping she was thriving with the natives. I thought of all the girls who had fallen along the trail, their graves either marked with hastily made wooden crosses or not marked at all. I struggled to recall some of their faces, especially the girls who had succumbed to death and disease in the very early weeks of the journey.

I prayed for the peace of their souls as my brain finally released me to slumber.

San Francisco

ITHOUGHT ABOUT MARTHA FOR the majority of the next day. I regretted not making an effort to say goodbye. I hadn't even thought to. I was just so consumed with packing up and departing town that I hadn't even given one solid thought to my dear friend. I could rely on the peace I had regarding her contentment. I felt that Martha was in good hands. She had a kind, caring man; a new family; and her own home and farm. I felt that I was leaving her behind in her own world of paradise.

The landscape was beautiful on this portion of the trail. A vast desert stretched to snow-peaked mountains. It was magnificent, easily the most stunning part of America I had seen yet. This land was far more interesting to look at than the constant rolling grass of the Plains. I had seen enough plains, grassy meadows, and endless crops to last me several lifetimes.

Per usual, Paul talked all day long. No one seemed to tire of his rambling. It provided us a source of escape and entertainment. It was far more interesting to listen to Paul tell his tall tales than to listen to the moaning of the livestock or creaking of the wagons.

Paul remained respectful of my wishes. Of course, he would reach for my hand and steal kisses to my cheeks whenever he could, but he never again mentioned marriage, babies, or growing old together. I was relieved. I was completely opposed to any such notion, angered at the concepts due to my repeated dreaming of them with the likes of Zechariah. Despite my anger toward him, a part of me missed Zechariah, and I felt a deep sense of fear and lacking that I would never see him again.

The days grew longer, and the heat intensified. There was no springtime in the desert, only the relentless rays of the sun. The air dried, evaporating any pleasant moisture from the breeze. Instead, we were left with an oven-like blast of constant heat that blazed the skin and stung the eyes. I would walk with my eyes closed for vast portions of the day, the sun and sand battering my face in unison.

The land grew even drier, and the air was now nearly unbearable. We were in the final stretches of the trail. Several weeks, perhaps a month, since we had left Great Salt Lake City, the journey had become almost impossible. Walking beside the marching mules was arduous at best and completely unmanageable at worst. Paul was kind and allowed me to ride in the wagon during the peak hours of the day. I had never experienced anything as difficult as this portion of the trail.

The desert was ruthless and never-ending. Day in and day out, we seemed to cross nothing but barren sand, colorless rocks, and a wasteland of petrified salt beds. I would manage to walk during the later afternoon hours. I tried to ignore the half-decayed carcasses of the fallen livestock of earlier wagon trains. Many had been there for months, years even. I even saw several bits and pieces of what appeared to be human remains, stripped and scattered by the elusive desert wildlife.

The nights were long and cold and the days endless and grueling. Several of the wagoners collapsed due to the heat. As far as I knew, we hadn't lost anyone yet. Thankfully, the train was well-prepared with a stockade of contained water. Still, the heat was so tangible and cruel that it was very hard to imagine we were going to make it across this vast landscape of dried, heated nothingness intact.

We marched and marched. Even Paul had fallen silent. I heard mumblings of lost comrades. We never stopped to bury anyone, at least, not that I ever noticed. If true, I shuddered to think that the fallen were simply left where they had taken their last breaths, left to rot and decay in the sun, food for the night creatures of the desert and visual warnings for the wagon trains yet to come.

We marched and marched. Day in and day out. The earth grew hotter; the miles winded longer. Nothing. Sun. Dirt. Sand. Nothing. Heat. Relentless.

Finally, after what felt like several months but was perhaps no more than a month and a half at best, we made it to the first of the active California gold mines.

The landscape had finally relented, leaving the barren sand for colorful rocks and canyons. Tall trees towered toward the heavens. Fresh streams trickled and twinkled nearby.

I was relieved to finally be free of the trail, but too depleted of energy or excitement to fully enjoy our destination. It took me days to recover, days spent lying in and out of consciousness in the back of one of the wagons. The rest of the convoy had separated and established themselves in either new camps or with ones that had already existed but were welcoming to new arrivals. Around the fifth day after our arrival, I finally felt well enough to leave the wagon and seek some familiar faces. I found Paul and several other young men from our train hard at work beside a group of strangers. No one noticed me. Each simply focused on their task, a repeated digging and sifting through the dirt. I watched quietly for a while before returning to the wagon for food and water. I remained there until Paul and some of the other boys returned for a break.

They ate in silence, even Paul. I did my best to serve them, breaking bits of dried bread and meat onto small tin plates. I filled their cups with water, which they quickly gulped down. They returned to the mine without a word.

* * *

The next day, I was directed by one of the older men of our convoy to go down to the creek. I was given a pan and assigned to sifting. Sifting. Sifting. Sifting. Hours and hours, I did nothing but sift. There were a few other women here, much to my surprise, but mostly there were men as far as the eye could see. Speaking was left to a bare minimum. Everyone focused their energy on constant work.

Paul and many of the others worked the cradles, a far larger and faster way to sift the waterbed. The youngest males and handful of females were relegated to the creek side, forced to endure the most tedious form of mining with little to no results. I never saw a single speck of gold. Never. The bottom of my pan only turned up bits of stone and rubble that were heavier than the rest of the sediment.

It seemed the others were no luckier. No one spoke in the evenings. Everyone was too exhausted. We just slept, woke to feed, and worked. We worked from sun up till sundown. Day in and out. No breaks. Finally, after about three and a half weeks of sifting through nothing but sand, dirt, and rocks, I approached Paul.

"I want to go to San Francisco," I declared, watching him as he poked at his cornmeal in silence. "I don't want to stay here."

Paul ignored me.

"Paul?" I said in a raised voice.

"Fine," he finally replied. "But I ain't goin' with ya. None of us are. We have too much work to do."

I stared for a moment, unsure if I wanted to venture into such a foreign place alone. I thought for a long while before finally responding.

"'Fine," I said in an assured tone. "Can I leave with the next train?"

"Sure, fine," Paul answered without ever lifting his eyes. It was clear that the weeks of back-breaking labor with little to no return had taken its toll on him greatly.

The next evening, I joined one of the several wagon-long caravans headed to San Francisco. Many miners preferred to stay within the city limits for short breaks and supply replenishment or replacement. Only the most resilient remained in the fields without rest.

I was still and quiet as the wagon train journeyed the busy pathway toward San Francisco. The wagon was full. No one walked beside the wagons or livestock the way they did when out on the trail. No one had the energy. Everyone here was far more wiped of health and vigor than even when enduring the hardest portions of the months-long journey over the California Trail. The difference now was that they no longer had the inklings of hope to thrive on. Weeks of desperate mining with little return had wiped most of the gold dust-laden dreams right off the faces and out of the eyes of every gold-seeker here.

After several hours, we finally pulled into the edge of San Francisco. The city was like no place I had ever seen before. Even more so than St. Louis, the streets were bustling with people. Wagons and carts filled the roadways; people crowded the walkways. Wooden houses and buildings stretched for as far as the eye could see. The sounds and smells were like nothing I had ever encountered before.

My heart raced in nervous anticipation. I suddenly felt so alone and disconnected from anything and everything I knew as normal and familiar. I began to miss Martha.

The wagon stopped and the passengers departed. I remained seated, anxious and scared about what to do next. What was I thinking venturing into such a vast and bustling city all alone? Perhaps I should go back and remain with Paul and the others? My thoughts and worries spun ceaselessly in my head.

"Ya need to get out, hon?" a male voice boomed. I looked up to see the man who had been steering our wagon peering at me from the backside of the wooden vessel.

I nodded and scooted toward the edge of the cart.

"Where ya headin'?" the man asked, offering his hand to assist me down from the back of the wagon.

"I'm not sure," I heard myself answer.

"Ya gonna be okay out here all alone in this big city?"

I met his eyes with a fearful stare.

"Would you like me to escort you someplace?" he continued, obviously reading the terror in my eyes.

I failed to respond. I didn't know what to say. I was totally and honestly overwhelmed by the enormity of movement and action that went on around us. I had never seen so many people together in one place at one time, especially in the dead of night. I felt I had to struggle to catch a breath, the air used and overworked by the countless lungs pulling from it for oxygen.

"Come," the man said, tipping his hat toward a nearby building. "Let's go get us a drink."

I didn't say a word as I followed the man through the front door of the establishment. Inside, the voices of the loud and excited crowd suffocated the air and assaulted my ears. Men were everywhere.

Throughout the crowd, several women, colorfully yet hardly dressed, sprinkled through the males, many of them sitting atop the laps of their very eager and willing hosts.

I followed the man to the bar. He ordered two drinks and we waited.

"So," the man began, "tell me about yourself."

I managed to pull my eyes away from the alien scene around us and focus on his face. He had long hair, well beyond his shoulders, and a large, bushy beard to match. His eyes were friendly, the type of eyes that always seemed to smile. His hands were large and dirty, his clothes plastered with white sediment. It was clear he had just come from weeks of mining.

"My name is Meredith," I managed to say in a meek voice.

"I can't hear ya, hon," he replied, leaning his head closer to my face.

"Meredith," I said again, this time in a near shout. Even then, my voice could barely be heard above the constant roar of the room.

"Nice to meet ya, Miss Meredith," the man said, pulling his head back so he could again look at my face. "My name is Robert Thomas. From Missouri."

My eyes widened.

"I'm from Missouri as well," I said, my voice finding a far more natural volume and tone.

"Is that a fact?" the man asked, smiling. "Well, it is certainly nice to meet a fellow Missourian."

I felt at ease with this man. He was at least ten to fifteen years older than me. As our conversation continued, I learned that he had a wife and two children back in Missouri. He had journeyed the six-month trek to California with the promise to return to his family with untold amounts of wealth and gold along with him.

Nearly two years later, he was still mining, still far short of the wealth and riches he had come here for. The reality of limitless goldfields had been a fortune maker for only those who had first arrived in '48 and early '49. For those still digging, the promise of precious gold had been met by only a few select fortunate or those wealthy enough to hire other miners to dig for them. Slowly, private diggers had become paid laborers for larger companies who could scour the land faster and more aggressively. Many had left lucrative farms and businesses back East to now work for a poor and petty wage. Still, they continued to dig, fearing that giving up would be just one day shy of the big strike.

We finished off several shots of whiskey before making our way back out to the busy dirt roadway. The sight of so many people, livestock, and wagons moving all at once was still overwhelming to my senses. I still felt it difficult to catch my breath. I followed Robert back to the wagon we had arrived in.

"Well, miss," Robert said, pulling a large sack from the wagon, "I'm off to the boarding house. I need a bath and a good night's sleep."

I smiled and nodded, the heaviness of the whiskey still bubbling in my stomach and weighting the feeling of my head.

"Where're ya plannin' to sleep tonight?"

I looked around. The glowing lights from the countless nearby windows filled the air with an eerie orange hue.

"I'm sure I'll manage," I replied, keeping my eyes out over the still-bustling street. It had to be nearly midnight, yet the city was still fully awake and alive. I truly had never seen anything like it.

I could feel Robert staring at me.

"Meredith, I don't want to be out of line here, but I think it may be best if ya just stay with me for the night."

I brought my eyes to his. As before, the same warm smile defined his gaze.

"I—"

"I insist, hon," he interrupted. "I don't think ya really realize what a large place this is. This city has grown by the thousands over the last year or two. There are people here from all walks of life. Mostly men. I just don't feel right leavin' a young, innocent thing like you out here to fend for herself. I promise I ain't got any ill intent. I just won't be able to rest easy knowin' you're out here alone."

I wanted to argue; I wanted to walk away, but I couldn't. Defeated by my own fear and uncertainty, I agreed to join Robert at the boarding house. He paid the clerk for my stay, and we were led to a small room in the back of the house. There was a single bed, a small table, and a worn and tattered floor rug.

"You take the bed, Meredith," Robert announced, dropping his heavy, tan-colored sack onto the floor. "I'll take this here rug."

"No," I shook my head. "I couldn't possibly be such a burden. You paid for this room, this bed. You need your rest. I'll be just fine—"

I stopped talking when Robert placed his large hands softly against my face.

"I insist," he said, his warm eyes reflecting my worried expression. "I been sleepin' in the dirt and muck so long that a nice floor rug is no less than a king's bed to me. You are the lady of the room, so I insist you get the bed."

He nodded and patted the top of my head.

I moved to the corner and removed my skirt and blouse. I placed them over the sole wooden chair that stood vacant and alone in the room's farthest corner. In just my layered undergarments, I slipped beneath the covers and positioned my body until I felt comfortable. The weight of a hundred nights of sleeping on the ground or in the backside of a wagon lifted from my bones. Even the bed the Bethels had provided was not this soft and comfortable. My body dropped into the puffy softness of the mattress, releasing the tension of my overworked and aching muscles. The hours of sifting through dirt and sand flashed before my eyes as my brain settled into slumber. I slept soundly. I didn't wake at all during the night, and when my eyes finally peeked open in the early hours of dawn—the soft morning light seeping in through the shabby curtain of the room's only window—I saw Robert, still asleep on the floor rug, his face motionless and peaceful. Perhaps it was my fear of the unknown; the enormity of the city; or my plain mental, emotional, and physical exhaustion, but I felt safe with this man—peaceful.

It was almost as if I had known him my entire life.

Gold

R
OBERT REMAINED IN SAN Francisco for two days. During that time, he restocked his food and supplies and reloaded his wagon to return to the gold mines. He planned to start a new dig at a recently discovered riverside shore. There was word that several had found surface gold, and just a quick dig below the bedside sand would result in an even more easily accessible bounty. Robert planned to take his chances.

Robert didn't force me, but he offered to take me with him. He also offered to pay for a week's stay for me here at the boarding house. I weighed my options and decided to join him at the new dig site. I could tell he was relieved at my decision. During our two days together, Robert was a perfect gentleman. He always called me *hon* or *miss*; he opened doors for me, always made sure I was settled with a meal and drink before he would touch his own, and continued to insist that I sleep in the bed while he remained cuddled up on the worn and dirty floor rug.

As we followed one of the major roadways from the heart of the city, the traffic of people, animals, and wagons thinned to nothing. Soon, we were alone, a single wagon on the trail toward a new promise of found gold. It would take us two days to reach the new dig site.

Along the way, Robert spoke lovingly of his family back home. He and his wife had been childhood sweethearts. They married young but waited several years before having their children. I could tell he deeply loved his wife. The way his face would light up as he spoke of her, his warm and friendly eyes glazing with the teary mist of memory. My heart ached for him. He didn't say it, but it was clear to anyone that he greatly missed his family. I could almost touch the hand of his entity-like loneliness.

When we finally arrived at the new site, Robert mumbled something under his breath. The shoreside of the river was completely packed with miners. For as far as the eye could see, there was nothing but digging men, tents, and wagons. A large group of livestock filled a nearby meadow. Obviously, the rumor of the new surface gold had attracted the ear of hundreds.

Robert managed to find us a vacant lot along the northern-most section of the shore. Just behind us, the river swept into the captivity of two large mountains. The bit of shore in front of us was the last piece of flatland before the landscape surged upward along the side of the towering mountain rocks.

I helped Robert set up the tent. Within an hour, we joined the others at the shallow edge of the raging river, dipping our pans into the cool water below.

For three days straight, we did nothing but sift. Farther up the shore, some miners had installed a cradle and were hard at work managing through the river bed far faster than the rest of us. From what we could tell, no one was finding much of anything. Once again, the rumor and promise of precious gold had been nothing more than inflated words and slowly unraveling disappointment.

Each night, I lay beside Robert. He always fell asleep quickly, his loud and thunderous snoring lulling me to sleep. He never tried to touch me. He never even looked at me in the way so many other men had. He treated me with kindness and respect. I felt more like his daughter than just some strange girl who shared nothing more in common with him than being born and raised in the same state.

***

Just as the sun had begun to set the following evening, the shimmering glimmer of gold filled my pan. I stared at it for several seconds before managing a breath. It wasn't much, but it was certainly gold. It glittered in the faint fading of the sun like starlight. Noticing my sudden pause, Robert looked up at me, his face frozen as his eyes locked on the twinkle in my pan. He trudged through the water toward me.

"That's the most I've ever seen," he whispered, yet his voice high and excited. "That's at least three hundred and fifty dollars' worth!"

My hands began to shake, causing the rare and elusive metal to softly rattle against the tin.

"Quick," Robert nodded, never attempting to take the pan from me. "Let's get it to the tent."

I watched as he secured the glorious find in a small satchel that was sewn into the backside of his sleeping bag. He smiled as he hugged me. I could feel him shaking; the shock of finally striking gold was both exhilarating and frightening. If any of our fellow miners got word of what I had discovered, our lives would be in very real grave danger.

That evening, Robert was quiet. He didn't speak much as we ate. Normally, he would fill the night air with his warm and colorful stories of his life back home, things his wife or children had said or done, or tales of the boyhood adventures he had enjoyed with his own father. Tonight, he hardly uttered a word.

Robert slept with his shotgun laid over his chest. Unlike other nights, he didn't fall right to sleep. It was at least two hours before his snoring filled the tiny space of the canvas tent. I barely slept myself, even when Robert's powerful snoring urged my brain to allow it to lull me to sleep. The adrenaline of the gold discovery surged through my veins in an endless rush.

The next morning, Robert gave me a handful of money, telling me to venture down the shoreline toward the supply tents. As with most dig sites, several vendors set up tents, selling tools, food, and other goods to the laborious and weary miners. Much of what they sold was grossly overpriced, but unless a miner could afford to venture in and out of San Francisco on a weekly basis, he was forced to pay the high prices of those clever enough to take advantage of the overbearing isolation. Even those who did manage to make it to San Francisco more often were still not immune to the price gouging. Prices were a bit more reasonable due to the competition in the city, but compared to what these same goods and items would cost back East, vendors were making a fortune.

Robert instructed me on what to buy. I made a mental checklist and went on my way. I wasn't sure what everything would cost, but he seemed to have given me far more than I would need. It took a good hour or more to make it to the supply tents, and by the time I had secured the goods, filled the two sacks Robert had provided, and lumbered my way back toward our camp, nearly three hours had passed.

It took my brain several minutes to understand what had happened. Although the tent and campfire pit remained, the wagon was gone, its deep and obvious ruts snaking through the riverbed sand and toward the nearby grassy meadow. I returned the sacks to the tent and peered inside. Only one sleeping bag remained—mine. Robert's was gone. Near the fire, there was another sack, smaller than the two I had just dragged across the crowded shore. Inside was food, enough to last several weeks. The supplies I had just purchased would ensure survival in the mines, and the extra money would extend what was needed for even longer.

Robert had abandoned me here. While I was gone, he had secured his mules, ensured a lot for my survival, then pulled his wagon from the dig site with my small fortune in gold along with him.

Robbed

I WENT ABOUT THE NEXT two days as though everything was normal. I spent the daylight hours panning at the river's edge, keeping to myself, eating in silence during my two meal breaks. The other miners didn't seem to notice me much, until the third day.

Numerous times throughout the blazing hot afternoon, I caught several nearby miners pausing in their labor to gawk and stare at me. I imagined they had noticed that Robert was no longer around. I was alone and vulnerable—the only female in a seemingly endless sea of men.

That night, as I lay awake alone in the tent, my mind rotating the same ponderous questions regarding what I was going to do next, I heard voices approaching. There was more than one voice. It sounded like three. Every word was whispered.

I sat up and started to crawl toward the opening in the tent flaps, when three men snatched open the canvas and slid into the small space. I opened my mouth to scream, but the closest man covered my mouth, his hand thick with the muck of the nearby river. Another man pulled my legs down and apart. The third forced me onto my back. My heart raced; my mind echoed with the screaming of my inner voice. I saw flashes of red. An anger and rage I had never known before lifted my body from the tent floor and into a full stand. I could feel the men desperately trying to force me back to the ground, the sudden might of my strength and ability to overpower them both alarming and unexpected. Even I could not believe I had managed to stand to my full height with three adult men clinging to my legs like needy children.

I kicked and punched. I didn't even look or aim; I just swung my arms and legs around, knowing the slight distance between me and these invaders would ensure that I would strike at least one of them. I swung and kicked, my feet and hands thudding against several faces, necks, and upper bodies. I could hear the men shouting as they scrambled from the tent and back out into the night. I had warded them off before any of them had been able to accomplish what they had plotted.

The next morning, I packed the tent and supplies and walked off the riverbank toward the trail that would take me back to San Francisco. I glared at several of the men who looked my way as I passed them. I wasn't sure which of these weak and pathetic souls had tried to attack me the night before, but I met each of their curious looks and stares with the same cold glare. I dared any of them to try to repeat what had been attempted the night before.

I walked for miles before seeing another soul. I didn't have a plan. It had taken Robert and me two days to reach this dig site by wagon, so it would take at least five or more for me to make it back to the city by foot. The only passersby I saw were wagons heading to the overcrowded dig site. No one was heading back to San Francisco.

I rationed my food and water and walked far off the path before setting up my tent for the night. I didn't want to risk another encounter like the one that had driven me from the dig site. On the third day after I had vacated the riverside, a single wagon approached from behind. It was headed by a sole young man headed back to San Francisco. Naturally, I was wary of his offer to give me a ride back to the city, but my instincts told me I could trust him, although they had been clearly wrong about Robert.

The young man's name was Daniel Brewer. To my surprise, he was a Saint. Apparently, not all Saints remained in Great Salt Lake City. Some completed the trek west, intent on finding riches that would benefit their home, church, and people. Daniel was one of these Mormon gold-seekers; he had ventured here with two of his brothers. The brothers were still digging at the river, while Daniel made the weekly journey to San Francisco for food and supply replenishment. I felt safe when Daniel told me he was a Saint. From my experience, I knew he would not attempt to molest nor harm me in any way.

***

After another day and a half, we made it to San Francisco. Once again, the sights and sounds stole the air from my lungs and caused my head to spin.

Daniel dropped me off in the center of the city, not far from the boarding house where I had stayed with Robert. With two large sacks on my back and the smaller satchel tied around my waist, I walked the streets of San Francisco, blending into the constant flow of similarly clad people, mostly men. The few women I did see where either the wives of gold-seeking husbands, independent business owners, or prostitutes. Unlike the enslaved girls on the trail, these women were bold and brazen in their appearance. Most wore colorful, revealing costumes that certainly set them apart from their non-sex worker counterparts. None of the working women appeared to be captive or forced. It seemed they were here by choice, and proudly flaunted the excess of their sudden riches. With such a large population of mostly males, the need for female companionship was as in demand and lucrative as the food and supply vendors.

Eventually, I came across a section of the city that was primarily made up of tents. I scouted the landscape until I found an empty plot, close enough to the others to blend in, but far enough away to keep what I felt was a safe and secure distance. I set up the tent and unpacked my necessities. I warmed my food over a small fire and watched the California sun set over the nearby city. The other tent inhabitants kept to themselves and never paid me much mind.

That night, there was a terrible thunderstorm. The thunder pounded so loudly that I could feel it in the earth beneath the tent. The canvas rattled and shook in the wind. I feared it would tear or fly off the wooden poles altogether, but it remained in place.

The next morning, I packed my things and walked the streets, looking for any place that may be hiring. I passed several houses where obvious women of the night congregated on the front porches, seductively straddling the railings and banisters as if they were riding an animal. They would peer at me as I walked by, obviously curious about this sole, filthy female with a mountain of supplies strapped to her back.

I settled the large sacks and midsized satchel on the ground in a small alleyway. I tucked behind them so I could relieve myself. Just as my body began to dispel its waste, I felt the packs rise from behind me and disappear. Before I could even turn around, they were gone, leaving only the echo of shuffling, running footsteps bouncing against the wooden walls of the closest buildings. I now had nothing—not a single scrap of food nor supply to my name. Thankfully, I had tucked the cash Robert had given me against my bosom, so I at least had some money, but the tent, digging supplies, food, and cooking materials were all gone, lost to and stolen by some unseen thief.

I didn't cry. I showed no emotion at my deepening distress. I returned to the street, hopeful to see the person who had lifted my supplies, but realistic that they were more than likely long gone from the area.

I found a discarded crate of rotting lemons near the side of what appeared to be an eating establishment. I stuffed as many as I could into my skirt pockets and various nooks and crannies of my undergarments. The juice of the bitter citrus dripped down my chin and over my bosom as I sucked one of the near-rotted fruit from its skin. That was the only sustenance I had for the remainder of the day.

That night, I found a small crawlspace beneath the front porch staircase of what I assumed was a house. I tucked underneath it and curled myself into a tight ball, falling fast asleep until the dawn.

House Girl

IT WAS THE SOFT touch of a gentle hand that woke me the next morning. I looked up to see a young female, a very pretty girl garbed in a peach-colored dress, her hair piled high in a tower of bright blonde curls, her cheeks pink with powered blush, and her lips crimson red with painted-on lipstick.

"Are you okay, miss?" she asked in a high, sweet voice.

I looked around; the sunlight behind her illuminated the busy San Francisco street.

"You're under the front porch steps of the house I live in," she continued, her sparkling-blue eyes never moving from mine. "Would you like to come inside and get yourself cleaned up?"

I nodded, unsure if I should trust her. Still, after the hell I had just been through, the suggestion of a warm bath and perhaps an even warmer meal sounded like a pure slice of heaven.

She helped me as I crawled out from under the front porch, and I followed her up the stairs and into the house.

The foyer was quaint yet elegant. Fancy paintings adorned the walls; expensive-looking area rugs covered the wooden floors. Rose, the girl who had woken me, filled the air with the story of her life. I followed her to a small bathroom. Inside was a large porcelain tub, far fancier than any of the similar tubs I had cleaned in my days as a housemaid back in St. Louis. Rose filled the bath from a kettle, the warm water causing a pillar of steam to rise into the air and fog the small space. She remained in the room as I undressed and slipped beneath the surface of the inviting water. She continued to speak about her life as she dropped soap pellets into the water, which caused the bath to fill with multicolored bubbles. It was by far the most elegant bath experience I had ever encountered.

Rose was a prostitute, or *lady companion*, as she referred to herself. She had arrived here by boat. Having worked as a lady companion in New York City, she had enough money to afford the fare from the East Coast of the United States, around the southern-most tip of South America, and to the San Francisco Coast of California. It was a seven-month journey, even longer than that of the California Trail, but many—those who could afford it— preferred the sea-bound passage versus the arduous and dangerous journey across the American landscape. Of course, the voyage by sea had its own collection of diseases and moral perils, but it was a preferred method of travel for many well-to-do gold-seekers. The other girls who resided in this house were also lady companions. Several were from Paris; they had embarked the treacherous voyage over the various oceans, hoping to free themselves of their madams and pimps and carve out a life of their own in the promise of new business opportunities provided by the discovery of American gold.

"We have a madam of sorts," Rose confessed as she stirred the bathwater with her finger. She sat herself in a nearby chair, scooting it to the edge of the massive porcelain tub, offering me cloths and brushes for my personal bathing. I didn't find her presence to be odd. After months spent following defecating livestock and fellow filth-covered slave girls, I had little to no modesty left.

"Ms. Trudeau. She owns the house, but unlike the madams in New York, she doesn't manage us. We are independent workers here. We pay her room rent and abide by her house rules, but she doesn't get a cut of our profits. She runs a more refined house than many of the other brothels in the city. She prefers a more discreet and quieter clientele, not the drunken and often sickly souls that comprise most other companion houses."

Eventually, Rose asked me about my own life. She wanted to know why I was alone in San Francisco and what had led me to spend the night under the brothel's front porch steps. I provided her a slim and limited account of my abandonment in the goldfield and recent supply robbery. I didn't bother to mention my kidnapping and former captivity, although the lady companion thing was something we had in common. Of course, the circumstances surrounding my involvement were quite a bit different.

Rose helped me dry off, provided me a clean nightgown, and led me to the house's small kitchen. There, she prepared a small meal of scrambled eggs, bacon, and two slices of toast. She covered the toast with strawberry jam, the first sugary delicacy I had tasted in months. The Bethels preferred clean, bland foods. They didn't consume the fruit grown on their farm. They harvested and sold it along with their other various crops. I devoured the toast first, the sugary sweetness of the jam filling my mouth with the taste of splendor and delight.

"Ms. Trudeau will be home soon. She went to the market," Rose declared. "I hope you don't mind me telling her where I found you this morning. She won't take too kindly to some random street girl being in the house, but the fact that you took shelter under our porch should soften her to you a bit. No promises though."

An hour or so later, Ms. Blanche Trudeau arrived, a stout, stern-looking woman with a large bustline and wavy red hair. She looked to be about fifty years old, but her attire and painted face described that of a far younger woman.

"Who is this?" she asked as she freed her arms of several satchels of food.

"Ms. Trudeau, I'd like you to meet my new friend, Meredith," Rose announced, pulling my arm and offering my hand to the elder woman.

Ms. Trudeau stared at me with an inquisitive glint in her bright-green eyes.

"I found her under the porch steps this morning," Rose confessed. "She's had a bit of trouble recently. She's been robbed of the gold she discovered in the mines, and robbed of her few supplies, even food. I was hoping we could—"

Ms. Trudeau raised her right hand toward Rose, signaling for her silence. The girl obeyed immediately.

"Any interest in being a working girl?" she asked, keeping her intense stare locked on my face.

I shook my head slowly.

"No, ma'am," I managed to squeak, "I have no interest in that. I'll just get myself together and continue on—"

Ms. Trudeau raised her hand again, this time signaling for my silence.

"Can you cook and clean?" she asked, pursing her painted red lips.

"Yes, ma'am," I muttered.

"What's that? You need to speak up."

"Yes, ma'am," I said louder.

"We need a house girl. You will be up at dawn, serving breakfast to the girls, followed by a full cleaning of the entire house. The linens must be washed and changed daily. This is a service offered in the room rent for the girls, and I need some assistance in keeping things going every day. The job pays ten dollars a week."

My heart jumped at the number. Ten dollars a week was more money than what I managed to make as a housemaid in two months. It was clear that the profits of the lady companion business were far more than simply bustling here in San Francisco.

I agreed to Ms. Trudeau's terms and conditions. She ran a tight ship. Everything was precisely scheduled and executed. There was no room for playfulness or dilly-dallying. My job was on a trial basis. She would offer the position permanently if she was pleased and impressed during my probational period.

Rose squealed with excitement as she led me to her room.

"I just knew Ms. Trudeau would like you!" she beamed.

Upon closer inspection, beneath the bosom-bursting cut of her dress and the heavy-handed paints and powders of her face, Rose was not much older than Susie had been, the twelve-year-old from the slave train. I imagined Rose was no older than fourteen at most.

Rose offered me a plain brown skirt and beige shirt. It was clean but fit a bit tightly.

"I'm not sure if your old clothes can be saved," Rose laughed, holding up the muck-covered garments that had been on my back for months. "You can have what I gave you. I don't really need them anymore. Ms. Trudeau likes the girls of the house to wear elegant, colorful gowns, but nothing tawdry or gaudy, like many of the other worker girls do. I haven't worn what I gave you since I arrived here last year. Also, I am sure Ms. Trudeau will provide a uniform for you."

Slowly, the other girls began to awaken and strut into the hallway. Collectively, they were warm and friendly toward me. Each was dressed beautifully. They reminded me of the fairy-tale princesses from the stories I had heard as a child. Then, I ventured downstairs to join Ms. Trudeau in the kitchen, assisting her with the lunch preparations.

Once the evening set in, the men began to arrive. Unlike the tired, dirty men on the trail, these men were well-dressed, clean, and refined. These were not the back-broken miners from the fields, but the businessmen who owned the local shops or labor-funded mining companies. Most were older, although some appeared to be no more than thirty or so. They would speak briefly with Ms. Trudeau. It was clear that most had a rapport with her, so I assumed they were repeat customers with their favored girl. This was not much different than the trail customers, albeit far more comfortable, polished, and classy.

Once the men had disappeared upstairs, I followed Ms. Trudeau as she completed her evening chores. I did my best to keep up with her. She never said too much to me, only offering a few helpful instructions when I did something not quite up to her liking or standard.

Well after midnight, Ms. Trudeau showed me to my quarters, which were inside the grand staircase's broom closet. The space was tiny but safe, quaint, and surprisingly comfortable. The small cot had a quilt and pillow, and without a window to filter unwelcome light from the lamp-lit city street, the blackness of the closet pulled me into a deep and immediate sleep.

For the first time since leaving the Bethels, I felt truly safe and able to rest.

Caroline

BEFORE THE SUN HAD fully risen over the nearby houses and buildings, Ms. Trudeau woke me from my sound sleep. We stripped the beds as the girls ate their breakfast in the kitchen. We changed the linens with those that had been washed and hung to dry the previous morning. We hand-washed the sheets from the prior night and hung them on the wire clothesline that crossed the entire length of the relatively large backyard. The girls tended to their own tasks of self-maintenance and pampering. They took turns in the bath, offering to scrub each other's back or wash one another's hair. Once dried and dressed, they would paint each other's nails and faces. They would whisper and giggle in the sitting room or read aloud from one of Ms. Trudeau's library of countless books. I minded my business and completed each task given to me with precision and accuracy. I didn't want to upset Ms. Trudeau in any way. As each day blended into the next, I realized just how much I really did need this job. The pay was enormous for an uneducated and relatively unskilled woman, the quarters safe and clean, and the food hearty and fulfilling. I would be a fool to somehow mess this up and lose this gifted opportunity.

My probationary period ended, and Ms. Trudeau offered me the position permanently. She paid me my first wages, which I tucked beneath my pillow, and praised me with kind words of gratitude and appreciation.

"If you ever change your mind," the elder woman spoke, adjusting her hair and eyeing her painted face in a nearby looking glass. "I always have a position open for a new girl. The money is much better. You could do incredibly well."

I blushed as she turned to face me, lifting her hand to my cheek.

"You're a very pretty young lady," she said, the once suspicious glint in her eye now calm and longing. I couldn't be sure, but it was almost as if she gazed at me lustfully, the way the nameless men on the trail had peered at us girls. I ignored the thought and continued tending to my chores.

The days rolled into weeks, which eventually gave way to months. I was assigned the market duty, which I did every morning right after breakfast. I was slowly becoming used to the mass of traffic on the streets. I no longer felt the need to catch my breath or hold onto nearby railings or walls when my head would begin to spin. Eventually, I had fully adjusted to city life.

The California days were starting to show hints of autumn. The morning and evening air were chilly, and the nights were downright cold. Soon, the winter would arrive, and the nearby miners would all seek more permanent shelter in the city. Ms. Trudeau said winters were the girls' most lucrative times. She continued to offer me a position as a working girl. I could make more money than I could ever dream of. Her room rent was reasonable, so I could save my money, or spend it on lavish gowns and gifts. Some of the girls were planning to open other businesses, either solely or in groups or partnerships. They were wise enough to know that their marketability as lady companions would last only as long as their youth and looks favored them. As soon as a girl reached a certain age and the evidence of time had begun to root in her face, her days as a working girl would be numbered. The wisest girls planned for the future. The immature and more opulent-minded ones simply spent their money carelessly, assuming they would eventually marry one of their clients and be cared for when they were too old for the trade.

I couldn't bring myself to take up Ms. Trudeau's offer. Despite months of forced prostitution on the trail and a time spent as a more independent worker in the weeks we girls had escaped our captors, I could no longer allow myself to be in the company of men in that way, despite the completely and vastly different circumstances. The work here wasn't forced, either by captors or need for survival. The men weren't sickly, and the room and board were clean and almost elegant. Still, no part of me wanted to return to using my body in the service of men. It had been months since I had been with a man in that way, and I never felt that I was lacking. I was comfortable and content in my duties as Ms. Trudeau's house assistant, and I was satisfied with the money I was making.

***

One morning, as I slipped through the San Francisco street toward the food market, my eyes caught sight of a familiar figure. Lost in the sea of strange and unfamiliar faces, I could have sworn I had caught sight of Caroline. I struggled through the crowd, but never found the girl I had seen. Perhaps it was just my imagination, or perhaps it was just a spilling over of one of my dreams. I often dreamt of Beth and Caroline, wondering where they were today. I also dreamt of Emma, seeing her as a native's wife, perhaps a mother to her own brood of babies.

I made it to the market and began to follow the list Ms. Trudeau had given me. It was then that I definitely saw her: Caroline, standing just feet in front of me, her face locked in my direction, her mouth open, her eyes wide.

"Caroline!" I cried, dropping my basket and running toward her. Before I could reach her, she spun on her heels and dashed into the fast-moving crowd. It was certainly her. I knew I had not dreamt or imagined it this time.

I returned for my basket and tried to find her but to no avail. I completed the shopping, returned to the house, and assisted with the lunch preparations, all the while obsessing over what had just occurred. Why had Caroline run away from me? What threat could I possibly be to her?

I went to sleep that night with the flashing image of Caroline's shocked and staring face filling the darkness behind my closed eyelids. I vowed to myself then and there, somehow, someway, I would find her again.

A Familiar Face

ISEARCHED DESPERATELY FOR CAROLINE each time I went to the market. Weeks went by, and I never caught sight of her again. Eventually, Ms. Trudeau started complaining about the amount of time it would take me to go and return from the market, so I had to limit my search time and focus on gathering what was on the shopping list and return home before Ms. Trudeau could grumble. It was at least two months after I had seen Caroline when another familiar face stunned my senses, paralyzing me in place at just the sight of their face: Zechariah.

He arrived at the front door one evening. Ms. Trudeau welcomed him in as she would any client, but he wasn't interested in hiring the services of any of the girls. He was on a mission, seeking a specific name: mine.

"Does a girl by the name of Meredith work here?" I heard his deep baritone boom from the foyer. I was in the kitchen preparing supper for the girls. I stopped what I was doing and crept toward the entryway of the house. To my shock, there he was, Zechariah, as handsome as ever. He didn't see me, but from my view in the shadowed corner of the hallway, I couldn't take my eyes off of him.

"I have a house girl by that name, but no working girl," Ms. Trudeau told him. "May I ask who you are, please, sir?"

"Just an old friend," Zechariah replied, scouting the room with his intense stare. "Would I be able to speak with her, please, ma'am?"

Ms. Trudeau didn't answer right away. I could tell she was trying to decide how to properly handle this situation. She prided herself on running a high-end brothel with quality clientele. There was no room for the riffraff or trouble caused by the poorer men who visited the cheaper establishments.

"Wait here a moment, please," she finally responded.

I dashed back into the kitchen before she could see me. My heart pounded wildly as I listened to the sound of Ms. Trudeau's fast-approaching footsteps.

"Meredith, dear," she said softly as she entered the kitchen. "There is a gentleman here that would like to speak with you. He says he is an old friend of yours."

I had to hold myself up against the counter; I was so frazzled and surprised that I felt faint. Ms. Trudeau could see that something was clearly the matter.

"Are you okay, dear?" she asked, stepping further into the kitchen. "You look quite flushed."

"I'm okay," I managed to whisper. "I just need some water."

I focused on my breathing while Ms. Trudeau fetched a glass of water. I gulped it down in one giant mouthful. The feeling of the mass of liquid as it channeled through my body was the substance needed to ease my frayed and rattling nerves.

"Okay," I said once I felt my heartbeat soften and my lungs settle. "I will see him."

I was light-headed as I followed Ms. Trudeau to the foyer. As the corridor morphed from darkness into the light of the house's entryway, I felt Zechariah's eyes fall over me for the first time in countless weeks.

"Meredith," I heard him say in a near gasp.

I looked up, the pounding of my heart seeming to move into my throat as my eyes met his. Despite the time and distance between us, just standing in his presence had the same physical effect over my body as it always had. I was still completely drawn to this man.

"How are you?" he asked, stepping a bit closer to me but keeping a comfortable distance for us both.

I could hear Ms. Trudeau slip into the nearby parlor. She would be close enough to hear the conversation.

"I've been looking for you for weeks," Zechariah admitted, his face suddenly soft and worried. "I never imagined I would actually find you. This city is so massive. I've never seen anything like it. Also, there are so many of these kinds of places here, I never thought—"

"You assumed I was working as a prostitute?" I interrupted, my voice soft and lacking air. I inhaled deeply to satiate my struggling lungs.

"Well," Zechariah scrambled, his normally stoic and stern eyes spinning in thought, "I just figured—"

"Well, I'm not," I retorted. "That life was forced upon me, as I have told you before. I am not involved in that now because now I have a choice. But even still, I do not judge the girls who openly and freely decide to work in that profession. They are kind, sweet girls. They've decided to make a life for themselves, and they do very well. It may not be up to your moral standards, but at least they are making an honest living. They aren't hurting anyone by what they are doing. They aren't wronging by stealing or cheating."

Zechariah only stared, his face lost in the fiery rage of my eyes.

"I'm sorry," he finally managed to say, his voice detailing his embarrassment. "I only thought . . ."

Wisely, he heeded the warning of my glare and stopped talking. As upset as I was, I still didn't want him to go. He was the first familiar presence I had seen in months, besides the brief glimpse of Caroline, of course.

"What are you doing in San Francisco?" I asked, easing the sudden tension of the room.

"I, uh, I . . ." Zechariah struggled to form his words. It was clear that my angry reaction had truly gotten the best of him. For once, he was wounded by my disdain and unacceptance of his limited and ongoing assumption regarding my choice, or lack thereof, as a sex worker. Perhaps now he could finally see that what happened to me on the trail was not the same as what was happening under the roof of this house.

"I came out here with some other Saints. We're here for six months, digging for gold."

"You came during the winter?" I queried, my head nodding slightly in curiosity.

"Well, yeah. I mean I guess we . . ."

Zechariah stopped talking and just stared at me.

"I came here alone," he finally admitted after a long moment of silent staring. "I came here to find you."

My heart skipped so many beats that I felt myself nearly fall to the floor. Zechariah noticed and closed the slight space between us.

"Are you okay?" he asked, his face pinched with worry.

"Yes," I whispered. "I just need to sit down a spell."

Zechariah led me into the parlor, where Ms. Trudeau was sitting, pretending to read one of her books.

"What's the matter?" she asked as Zechariah helped me to one of the floral-print sofas.

"She's feeling a bit light-headed. Am I able to fetch her some water?"

Ms. Trudeau just stared at Zechariah for what felt like several minutes before answering.

"I will fetch the water," she finally declared. "Just have a seat, sir."

Ms. Trudeau swept out of the room and into the kitchen. Zechariah sat beside me; the feeling of his large body next to mine was both exhilarating and nerve-racking. In the short span of less than thirty minutes, Zechariah spoke more words to me than he ever had in the months of knowing him both out on the trail and in Great Salt Lake City.

"You came all this way just to see me?" I finally managed to ask, easing the ceaseless tension in the air.

"Well . . . I . . . I was . . ."

He began to fidget, one hand spinning over the other, his knees bobbing from the movement of his feet.

"Yes," he finally replied, lowering the high tension in his voice with one simple word of truth.

I felt a tear fill my right eye, but I refused to show Zechariah any emotion. I needed more information.

"Why?"

"Why what?" Zechariah asked, turning his head to face me. I wiped away the rogue tear before he could see it.

"Why did you travel all this way . . . across the Sierra, the most dangerous portion of the trail, just to see me?"

"I needed to know you were safe."

My heart skipped at his response. I felt myself falling into the clarity of his eyes. Unless I was mistaken, I was sure he had done the same with mine. The energy between us was so alive, so tangible, that it felt like a third person sitting on the small sofa.

"Water, dear," Ms. Trudeau broke the intensity of the moment with her quiet and sudden arrival.

I took the glass from her hand and thanked her.

"Your gentleman friend will need to go now," Ms. Trudeau announced. "It's time for supper. The evening clientele will be arriving in just an hour or so."

I nodded my head without looking away from Zechariah. Our stares remained locked, connected, intense. I could hear a thousand words from just the look on his face, far more words than he would ever speak with his voice.

I walked him to the foyer and opened the door.

"When will I be able to see you again?" he asked, stepping out onto the front porch, the chilly air of the San Francisco winter greeting any portions of exposed skin.

"Tomorrow night," I heard myself say, the words exiting my mouth before consulting my brain. "Ms. Trudeau allows me Friday nights off. I usually just stay in and work on my studies. Ms. Trudeau is teaching me to write."

Zechariah smiled slightly, which, for him, was massive.

"I will be here tomorrow night, then."

I smiled and nodded before closing the door. Through the stained glass of the front door, I watched his shadow disappear into the night. My head spun and my feet felt unsteady as I made my way back to the kitchen. A silent, dormant part of me was alive again for the first time since leaving Great Salt Lake City.

As much as I chose to consciously deny it, I was in love with Zechariah, a pure and powerful feeling I had never once felt for any other man.

Zechariah's Confession

Z ECHARIAH ARRIVED PROMPTLY AT seven the next evening. In his hand: a single red rose.

"A rose," I commented as I joined him on the front porch. "I didn't think you thought of me as a female worthy of a rose."

"Just take it," he smirked, forcing the sole flower at my hand.

I returned his smile and took the thorny stem into my gloved fingers. With the money I was making working for Ms. Trudeau, I had managed to buy myself a few nice outfits. Tonight, I wore my favorite dress: a purple number with a lace-covered upper bosom. Unlike the flashier and more revealing gowns the other girls in the house wore, mine was simple and conservative, even more so than the matronly attire Ms. Trudeau insisted upon wearing. Around my shoulders was a heavy, layered shawl. My gloves matched the dress, which looked refined and elegant, but certainly did not do much to ward off the slightly bitter chill of the night air.

"Where are we going?" I asked Zechariah as we quietly strolled the street side. Unlike the nights of the warmer seasons, the streets were far less crowded during the winter. Granted, the San Francisco winter was nothing compared to the frigid temperatures of St. Louis or even Great Salt Lake City, but they were enough to keep people from dwelling in the streets when they didn't need to.

"I thought we could grab a bite to eat first," Zechariah started, quietly taking my hand in his. "Followed by a stroll along the docks. I like to look at all the ships. There are so many. I've heard it told that many are lacking return crews due to their original crews abandoning their nautical duties to try their luck out in the goldfields."

I was quiet as I listened, more focused on the warmth of his large and strong hand against my demure, gloved one. The feeling of him next to me ignited every fiber of my being. I was awake and alive in a way I could only describe as pure ecstasy.

Zechariah briefly spoke of the Saints I knew back in Great Salt Lake City. According to him, the Bethels had lost one of their children, Tabitha, the youngest daughter, to typhoid fever. My heart broke at the news. As much as my life with the Bethels had been subdued and boring, I still cared for the family and was devasted to hear of their tragic loss. Eventually, Zechariah mentioned Martha. For some reason, I had been afraid to bring her up.

"Martha is doing well," he shared. "She and her husband are expecting. The baby is due in the early spring. She's overjoyed. Something about being with child has removed her from her shell. She is quite involved in church services now. She's quickly becoming one of the top wives at the meetinghouse. Everyone really likes her."

I smiled at the news. I so missed Martha and longed for her friendship, but I knew her life was meant to stay in what was now known as the Territory of Utah. The United States government had denied the Saints their petitioned state of Deseret.

After several blocks of nonstop walking, we finally arrived at a small eatery on the corner of a busy intersection. Wagons and livestock filled the street, and hooded or heavily coated people went about their business. Inside the small dining room, only a few of the many tables were occupied. A large man, well dressed in a fancy suit, led us to the corner of the room. Zechariah ordered large plates of freshly caught seafood, a delicacy neither one of us had ever experienced before.

We chatted during the meal; Zechariah peppered the buoyant conversation with lighthearted jabs at some of the Mormon church elders. I was both amused and amazed at the accuracy of his imitations of these men. The way he would contort his facial expressions and alter his voice was truly uncanny. I couldn't get over how alive and animated Zechariah was. I had never once witnessed even a small glimpse of this side of him all throughout our time together in the past. It was as if a completely new person had overtaken his body and was now perusing the San Francisco streets in his skin.

With the delicious and satisfying meal through, we walked hand in hand along the dockside. Zechariah was right, the harbor was completely filled with countless ships. Most were large with grand and towering sails and masts, and others were small and almost invisible next to their grander counterparts. I assumed these were the fishing boats that ventured out to sea daily. The massive ships had carried countless gold-seekers who, along with the ship's crew, were either enduring the cold nights out in the gold mines or resting somewhere within the city limits.

We walked for miles, just roaming the San Francisco streets without concern of time or place. Zechariah was interested in my story of what had transpired since I had left Great Salt Lake City. I could feel his hand tense as I recounted the tale of Robert Thomas and how he had fled the riverside goldfield with the large sum of profit I had panned from the riverbed.

As we rounded the corner of the street that would lead us back to Ms. Trudeau's two-story brothel, Zechariah paused in his tracks and slowly turned me toward him.

"If it ain't already obvious," he began, his eyes flitting nervously in several directions. "I love you, Meredith."

As those glorious words rolled from his tongue—his eyes locked over mine, the reflection of my face staring back at me in the warm glow of the nearby lanterns—I lost my breath and began to struggle for air.

"Meredith?" Zechariah said nervously, moving his arms around my waist to prevent me from falling.

"I'm fine," I said in a breathless whisper. "I'm okay."

I managed to usher a large mouthful of brisk air into my quaking lungs and secure my expression over Zechariah's concerned stare.

"I love you, too, Zechariah. I have ever since the first time I saw you out on the trail."

He smiled and nodded.

"I know," he confessed, a sly glint in his eyes. "I could tell."

"Then why were you so cruel to me? Why did you shame me for something I had no choice nor control over?"

Zechariah paused for a while before finally answering.

"Because it's what I thought I was supposed to say," he confessed. "As a Saint, I was raised to believe that every sin is by choice. I couldn't understand how something so terrible could be imposed upon someone without their conscious involvement or without their participation. I was a fool, Meredith. It took me months of grappling with my own mind to finally understand that what had been done to you was not your fault. I finally understood that you didn't need repentance and forgiveness. You just needed freedom."

I melted inside at the sound of these words flowing from Zechariah's mouth. His honesty was something I could have once only dreamed about.

"Oh, what I'd like to do to those bastards who harmed you," he continued, his face darkening with the nearby shadows.

"The men I was with?" I asked innocently. "No, they were just doing what they paid—"

"No," Zechariah interrupted, his anger now radiating. "The ones who held you there. The ones who killed my family."

It was suddenly clear to me that Zechariah had not only ventured to San Francisco to find me, but to also track those who had murdered so many of his people yet remained uncaught and unpunished. I suppose he assumed they too had completed the journey west and were now a part of the vast and dense city populace.

I decided it was best to change the subject. I filled the rest of the journey with pointless conversation involving jokes I had heard the girls tell each other during their downtime in the parlor or shared the recipes I was learning while working with Ms. Trudeau in the kitchen. Zechariah listened, but I could tell he was still lost in the rambling of his disturbed mind. I hadn't thought too much about the fate of my captors, only the two dear girls I assumed they still had with them. Then it hit me: Caroline. If she was here, it was highly likely the captors were as well. I chose not to mention any of that to Zechariah. Not now, anyway.

My heart pounded loudly inside my chest as Zechariah grazed his lips over my gloved hand before bowing slightly. He promised to return tomorrow evening, even though I would not be free to go with him anywhere.

I dashed inside the house and to my tiny compartment beneath the staircase. I fell asleep that night for the first time in my life with the promise of love from a man I loved in return filling the ears of my memory.

I Want to Stay

ICOUNTED THE HOURS UNTIL I would see Zechariah again. I went about my daily tasks and chores in a sort of cloud or bubble. Hearing Zechariah's confessions of love was a sweet melody of song for my soul, a chorus that echoed in my head for the entirety of the day. Ms. Trudeau noticed the change in my demeanor and commented immediately.

"So, I take it you are smitten?" she asked as I prepared the lunch trays for the girls.

"I suppose, yes," I answered coyly.

"Does this mean you will be leaving me?" Ms. Trudeau continued, tapping her fingers on the countertop.

"Oh," I started, my words catching in my throat. "I don't imagine I will be going anywhere anytime soon, Ms. Trudeau. I am very happy here. Also, I really do need this job, and your pay is so very generous. I would never give that up so easily."

"What if this man asks you to marry him?"

The very thought of that proposition nearly brought me to my knees. Despite Zechariah's declaration of love, I hadn't even dreamed or fanaticized about him proposing. Perhaps it was an even more realistic possibility than I was willing to accept.

"I don't know, Ms. Trudeau," I managed to reply. "That seems like a long way off, if at all."

I could feel the elder woman staring at me from behind. Eventually, she tired of her interrogation and left the kitchen. It was just before the sun set and my allotted time with Zechariah loomed that she brought the subject up again.

"Just promise me you won't do anything stupid or sudden," she requested. "You're a smart girl. A hard worker. You could do very well in this town. You don't need a man behind you. Don't give up your potential just to be a barefoot, pregnant housewife."

She didn't wait for my response. She turned and moved into the parlor to join the waiting girls. The first clientele would be arriving at any moment. I composed myself and moved into the kitchen. With the dinner plates cleared, washed, and put away, I was free for an hour.

Zechariah arrived right on time. We sat on the front porch steps for every single minute of my one free hour.

"I'm looking for work here," Zechariah announced. "It's a lot harder than I thought it would be. I don't know any of these city trades. I've only ever known farming. If I don't find something soon, I'm gonna have to head back to Great Salt Lake."

He paused without speaking further. The silence between us suddenly became thick and heavy.

"If that happens . . ."

I waited on bated breath for him to continue.

"If that happens, Meredith . . . would you go back with me? I promise to do right by you. I'll make you my bride and—"

"No, Zechariah," I heard myself say without thought or preparation.

"Huh?" Zechariah mumbled, lifting his eyes to mine.

"I don't want to go back there," I continued. "The Saints are wonderful people, but I just don't belong there. I like my life here. I like the city. I've grown to love it. I don't want to live on a farm."

I could see the hurt in his eyes as my words filled his ears. I had never seen him appear so wounded before.

"But I came all this way for you," he spoke softly. "I can't just leave you here."

"Yes, you can, Zechariah," I replied confidently. "I know how to take care of myself. I know how to work and survive. I will be okay here."

"I understand, but . . . do you really want to live out your days working in a whorehouse?"

I felt a fire rage from my gut and into my brain. I opted to pause for a long moment instead of giving in to the sudden surge of pure anger.

"I love you, Zechariah. My God, I do. But I will not go back there. I will not leave San Francisco."

Zechariah looked away, his gaze trailing out over the dark street. I watched the reflection of passing people and wagons in his eyes as he contemplated what I had just told him.

"Fine," he finally said. "I will figure it out. I can't lose you."

I was stunned. These were not the words I was expecting to hear. I thought for sure he would become upset and walk away. I knew he wanted to return to Great Salt Lake City. It was clear that a country Mormon boy was a fish out of water in a big city like San Francisco. Still, his love for me reigned supreme, and he was willing to do whatever it took to stay.

Zechariah, always the proper gentleman, kissed my hand before walking off into the California night. I watched him until he moved out of sight, and then I returned into the house to complete my night chores, my stern and precise decision still rambling in my head. I was surprised at how certain I was about staying. A part of me would have believed I would have wanted to return to Great Salt Lake City with Zechariah. I would be with him, and I could see Martha. But something in me was content with my current life here in San Francisco; I felt a sort of soul-driven need to stay. I went to sleep that night knowing that my purpose here in this time and place had not yet been fulfilled.

Time would tell what that would be.

Beth

IWENT TO THE MARKET the next morning. Per usual, I spent the first fifteen minutes or so just cruising the busy stands, hoping for a glimpse of Caroline.

Just as I was paying for the fresh fruits that filled my basket to the brim, I caught sight of what I had only once glimpsed and what I had been seeking to see again for weeks: Caroline. She was dressed in a bright orange dress, moving along the walkway, her arms carrying two large baskets, both filled with market goods. I decided not to call out; that only scared her off the last time. This time, I remained silent but scurried the crowded walkway to catch up to her. Keeping a good distance between us, I followed her for blocks. Her orange dress was quite easy to spot amongst the sea of drab-clothed passersby.

Eventually, she turned down a narrow street—an alleyway—and entered the back door of a large house. My heart was pounding so wildly inside my chest that I thought I might fall over. I took a long moment to compose myself before walking past the alleyway and toward the street that would lead me to the front side of the house. As I neared closer to the front porch, I saw several colorfully dressed girls gathered on the steps and railings. It was clear this was another house for working girls.

As I approached, several of the girls took notice of me. I diverted my eyes in the opposite direction, not wanting to seem obvious or interested. It was then that I heard my name.

"Meredith!" a voice exclaimed. "Is that really you?"

I turned my head to see Beth—dressed in a bosom-hugging green dress, which had a skirt that revealed her stocking-covered legs—making her way down the front porch steps.

"Oh my God, I don't believe it! I simply cannot believe it!"

My heart raced as I set my basket down to accept Beth's exuberant embrace. In my complete shock, I felt a few tears escape my eyes and roll down my cheeks. From the stuttering rhythm of her chest, I could tell that Beth was also crying.

"I never thought I'd see you again!" Beth squealed, her face now smudged with tears and running makeup. "I thought you had drowned in that river!"

"Beth," I whispered, struggling to find my voice. "How did you . . . how are you . . ."

"I'm a working girl now!" she declared excitedly. "No more dirty, nasty men like out on the trail. The men here are much cleaner and gentler. I much prefer San Francisco to anything on the trail."

"But how are you . . . what about Caro—"

My head was spinning, my words stunted. The enormity of it all was nearly crippling.

"Oh, Meredith," Beth said softly. "Let's sit you down."

She guided me to the front porch steps of the brothel. I could hear the other girls hush as we approached. They were now quiet and listening.

"Caroline is here, too," Beth explained, understanding my previous cut-off questions. "So is Agatha. She runs this house. She—"

"Agatha?" I asked breathlessly, feeling my body tense at just the mention of her name. "What do you . . . why . . . ?"

"Oh, it's not like it was. She looks after us. She makes sure we are well taken care of."

I looked around nervously. The last thing in the world I wanted was to come face-to-face with an unexpecting Agatha.

"She shot Jeremy," Beth whispered into my ear. "Way back on the trail. Not long after we lost you and Martha."

She paused for a moment before asking excitedly, "Martha! Oh my God, is she here too?"

I shook my head and stood to my feet. I stumbled back to the basket, retrieved it, and started to walk toward the end of the block.

"Meredith!" I heard Beth cry. "Wait!"

I continued my rapid pace. I was too afraid to be anywhere near any place where Agatha might be. I had never imagined I would ever see her again, much less when I wasn't prepared to.

"Meredith!" Beth shouted, now winded. "Wait!"

She grabbed my shoulder, halting me in place.

"It's okay, Agatha won't hurt you."

I watched as the young girl struggled for air.

"My," she exhaled, "I haven't run like that in months!"

"I need to get going, Beth. It was very nice to see you. I—"

"Don't you want to come say hello to Caroline?"

It took me several long seconds to respond. Eventually, I heard my voice answering for me.

"No," I said softly. "I would like to see her. But not like this. Not now."

Beth just stared at me, a curious look frozen over her face.

"Oh, but it is so wonderful to see you again, Meredith!" she declared, squeezing me in her arms. "I have missed you so."

We said a casual goodbye, and I went on my way. I don't recall the walk home; I was completely lost in the raging flood of thoughts that now swept through my head. Beth and Caroline were working girls for Agatha, the sadistic, evil female captor? How was this possible?

I didn't stop ruminating for the rest of the day, and even when my head finally met my pillow, the endless sea of unanswered questions continued to churn and stir. It was nearly dawn when I finally felt myself ease into unconsciousness.

A New Fisherman

I DIDN'T SAY A WORD about seeing Beth and Caroline when Zechariah arrived the next evening. I listened as he told me of his day seeking work. A fishing boat captain had taken an interest in him after Zechariah had stopped to ask him an endless slew of questions. The captain appreciated his enthusiasm and offered him a job. In a week's time, he would begin daily fishing ventures out in the Pacific. It was long, hard work, but something Zechariah was looking forward to. I was happy for him. He seemed excited, and I was relieved he wouldn't be returning to Great Salt Lake City, at least, not yet, anyway.

"What's the matter?" he eventually asked when I failed to say much after he had concluded his news. "You seem very quiet."

"Oh," I said, clearing my throat. "I'm just a bit tired, is all. I didn't get much sleep last night."

Zechariah stared for a while before responding.

"Well, perhaps I should let you go, then. Maybe Ms. Trudeau will let you take the rest of the night off to rest?"

I laughed.

"I don't think so," I said, patting his cheek. "I love you, Zechariah. I'm so happy you found work. I'm glad it's something you're interested in. Who knows, maybe you'll be an even better fisherman than you were a farmer."

He chuckled.

"We shall see. I'm worried about being sick the whole time. I've never been on a boat before."

"Just think of it as a wagon on water," I said in jest. "You certainly know what it's like to ride on a bumpy, creaky old wagon."

We laughed together. It was so nice to have these intimate moments with Zechariah. He was such a different person now that he was away from the church folk. He was careless and free, excitable and naive. I was so attracted to this rare side of him.

I went inside the house and straight to my bed. Much to my grateful surprise, Ms. Trudeau never disturbed me. Perhaps she could sense my need for slumber.

The extra sleep was certainly welcome, as the next day would end up being one of the hardest of my entire life.

Captive

I COMPLETED MY MORNING ROUTINE and left for the market at least a half an hour earlier than I normally did. Instead of heading straight to the market per usual, I walked past it and to the street where I had seen Beth on the front porch of the brothel she worked at. The house was quiet as I passed. None of the colorful girls were congregated on the front porch. There was an air of silence and stillness surrounding the entire street.

Feeling bold, I rounded the corner of the block and slipped into the alleyway behind the row of large, two-story homes. I walked quietly until I reached the back door I had seen Caroline enter two days prior. The door had a small window, so I crept close to it and peered inside.

I saw Caroline, hard at work in the kitchen preparing food. She had on an apron atop another colorful dress, this one lavender. It was clear that, like me, she was the house girl of this brothel.

I shifted my empty basket in my arm and turned to exit the alleyway, but bumped into a figure: the short man.

My eyes widened and my heart raced as I saw my reflection in his eyes. His stare was just as wide, but as quickly as he realized who I was, he grabbed my wrist and pulled me toward the back door of the house.

"Stop!" I screamed. "Wait!"

Before I could manage an escape, he tossed open the back door and threw me to the kitchen floor. I looked up to see Caroline, her face in a state of shock, her mouth gaping. I struggled to stand but was kicked back to the floor. Before I could cry out, the short man slammed his foot into my stomach, causing all the air in my lungs to rush out in one uncontrolled whoosh.

"Agatha!" I heard him yell. My heart thudded so loudly inside my head that the rest of his yelling became echoed and muffled. I struggled to lift myself from the floor, when a heavy-footed pair of boots stepped in front of my face. I turned my head, peering upward, right into the dark, beady eyes of Agatha.

"Well," she cooed in her thick German accent. "Look who we have here."

I rolled onto my side and attempted to slither away, but I felt her lift me from the ground. Before I knew it, I was being carried down a dark corridor and through a small doorway. I could hear Agatha's pounding footsteps and the feeling of being lowered into the ground. We were descending a stairway into a completely darkened room.

I was tossed to the ground, and again the density of the floor as it met my body forced out the bit of air I held in my lungs. As I struggled to breathe, I heard Agatha fumbling in the darkness. She began mumbling in German until the room illuminated from the glow of a wall torch. I lifted my head to view a scene of absolute horror. In what appeared to be the house's windowless basement, several cages filled the gray brick walls. Inside, several girls huddled together in the corner, their bodies filthy and completely naked. To my further shock and surprise, there were several boys as well, perhaps just twelve or thirteen years of age, huddled with the pack of young females.

I pushed myself off my stomach and into a crawl position. I forced my breathless body to move as fast as I physically could toward the stairs. Before I could manage more than a few feet, Agatha pulled me into the air by my hair. I bellowed at the pain.

"You fucking little whore!" she screamed. "I still have the bullet in me, you devil bitch!"

She swung me around like a weightless rag doll, releasing her fistful of my hair, which allowed my body to sail through the air and into the side of one of the iron cages. I could see the naked bodies within trembling at the crashing sound.

"It is time you pay me back for what I have suffered because of you!"

Yanking me by the hair again, Agatha dragged me to the other side of the room. I could hear her fumbling with what sounded like keys before managing to open a squeaking iron door. She kicked and punched me before throwing me inside a separate cage from the others. She locked the heavy door and walked away. Her thunderous footsteps vibrated the entire room as she ascended back into the house above. The basement door was locked shut, and her booming footsteps moved into another part of the house. Her thick accent could be heard in the distance, her words inaudible but her tone exuberant and celebratory.

For the first time in months, I was again her captive.

The Table

It was several hours before I composed myself enough to scream. I screamed and screamed until the basement door was unlocked and a pounding set of footsteps moved down the stairs.

"Silence!"

Through the faint light of the wall torch, I could see Caroline, her face twisted in an odd expression of what appeared to be anger and sadness.

"Caroline!" I whispered. "Please. Let me out of here."

The girl who I had known for months and miles out on the trail now glared at me as if I was a stranger. I saw a slight flash of sympathy in her eyes before she pursed her lips and shook her head.

"This is your fate now," she stated coldly. "If you scream again, I will be forced to send Paco down here."

"Paco?" I asked in a near whisper.

"The short man," she answered. "My husband."

"What?" I scoffed, but she spun on her heels and swooped back up the narrow staircase.

Hours went by. When the wall torch finally burnt out, there was nothing but complete blackness. In the dark, I could hear the other prisoners, all moaning or crying. I whispered loud enough for them to hear me, trying to get their attention and gain some information from them, but none would respond.

After what felt like an eternity, the basement door was unlocked, and several pairs of footsteps paraded down the stairway.

"This one is feisty. Perhaps the feistiest. But she's a good lay. How do you want her? Face up or down?"

Agatha concluded her statement by firing up a handheld torch. Behind her stood three men, all dressed in expensive suits. Behind them was Caroline, busily lighting several wall torches and clearing off what appeared to be a table.

Without thought, I spit at Agatha, the large gob of saliva striking her cheek. Before I could even react, she lunged the hand torch at my face, singeing the corner of my hair.

"You little demon!" she screamed. "I will fucking kill you!"

The men behind her all smiled, their shadowed faces hidden by the lack of light in the room.

"But first . . . you will make me lots of money."

She handed her torch to Caroline, who now stood by her side. She unlocked the cage door and reached within. I bit as hard as I could possibly bite. The taste of Agatha's blood slipped over my tongue and down my throat. She wailed like a wounded ox.

I managed to back away, my face soaked by Agatha's warm blood. Caroline reached in and grabbed me by the hair. I struggled, but she was much stronger. Agatha composed herself, her right hand still gushing blood. Together, Caroline and Agatha dragged me to the center of the room. The large wooden table was now in full view. On top of the wooden slats were several chains, similar to the ones that had been used to shackle us to the wagons.

I tried to cry out, but something was shoved into my mouth, a cloth of some sort, it's thickness so heavy and dry that it sopped up all the blood and saliva from my tongue like a sponge.

I was slammed onto the table, my arms and legs spread, shackles placed around my ankles and wrists. My head was down, my face rubbing against the rough surface of the wood. I felt my clothes being torn from my body, leaving just my undergarments in place. I squirmed the best I could, but my limbs were stretched so tight that the core of my being was locked firmly in place.

One by one, the men took their turns with me. They never removed my undergarments, but they cycled themselves from my backside in a nearly rhythmic fashion. I could hear them breathing and moaning as they thrust themselves against me. For the first time in so many months, I was again a hapless victim to a cycle of sexual abuse and assault. I felt myself ease right back into the thoughtless realm I had carved out in my head so many weeks before. As if just yesterday, I slipped right back into that state of thoughtlessness as if it were my natural mindset, allowing me to lose all track of time.

Finally, I felt myself being unchained and dragged back to the cage. I saw the three men refasten their pants and follow Agatha up the basement stairs. Caroline locked the cage and rushed to follow them.

This would be my life from now on.

Hell

THE MEN WHO CAME to the basement were not like the men who I imagined visited the girls upstairs. There, I assumed, was just like the rest of the brothels found in San Francisco, with clean, willing working girls who had a set of standards on what they would and would not do. Based on the dress of the girls I had seen, this house, much like Ms. Trudeau's, catered to the men of a wealthier breed. Down here, though, in the damp, dark confines of the basement, the sickest and most perverted of the city's elite explored their darkest fantasies with the locked and helpless bodies of slave flesh. Each night, hour after hour, groups of men were led into the basement, their victim selected from the cage and locked atop the massive wooden table. In the dark, I could hear the young boys crying as several men had their way with them. I would never look into the faint light of the wall torches. I didn't want to see what I could hear. I didn't want to scar my brain with those deep and painful images. Sometimes, two girls were chained on top of each other, with several men going at them at once. The men always appeared very clean and well groomed. It was clear that these were perhaps the wealthiest the town had to offer, not to mention the most insidious and disgusting.

The days went by, but I could never tell what time of day it was until the basement door was opened and the men where marched downstairs—night after night after night after night. The terror here made the slavery of the trail seem like a dream. I actually wished I could go back. At least then, there was a sense of limited freedom. There were also the other girls to gain support from. Here, we were kept separated and silenced. Caroline would visit the basement twice a day to give us water and dried bread. We were fed just enough to keep us alive. Apparently, the men who paid for us wanted our bodies as sickly and broken as possible.

After what must have been more than a week, I saw Agatha and the short man drag one of the naked teenage boys from the adjacent cage, his lifeless body bobbing over the floor, his skin completely covered in black dried blood. I grimaced at the sight, but slowly grew accustomed to the hell of the basement.

The sound of the girls being struck and abused, both by our captors and the men who paid for their bodies, became the lullaby of my nights. After my turn had passed and I was tossed back inside my cage, I would curl myself into a ball and fall asleep to the grotesque sounds that filled the humid air. The smell of defecation, both from the prisoners and the clients, filled the air with an awful stench. I grew used to the men urinating on me. That was common. But I could never really get used to their defecation. I fell asleep many a night with the warm, wet press of some strange man's shit splattered across my backside. Like pigs in filth, we were never bathed and never cleaned. Sickness and infection spread like wildfire.

***

One night, hours after a typical round of terror, I awoke to the sound of footsteps quietly approaching. I didn't move, but I lifted my head enough to peer into the darkness. It was Beth, carrying a small torch, her pretty face glowing in the flickering dark yellow of the flame.

"Meredith!" I heard her gasp, covering her mouth from both shock and, I assumed, the awful stench of the room. "It's true," she whispered, keeping her hand over her mouth as she slowly approached my cage. "Why have they done this to you? What did you do?"

I didn't understand her question. What did she mean, *what did I do*? I didn't do anything. None of us did. No one deserved to be down here.

"I'm so sorry, Meredith," she cried, her tears twinkling in the torchlight. Before I could manage a verbal response, she was gone, her feet pattering up the stairs, the sound of keys jingling as she locked the door. I was surprised she had been able to free the keys from Agatha to get down here.

It was then that the idea of escaping entered my mind.

Together Again

INEVER SAW BETH AGAIN. Days, weeks, perhaps a month had passed, and still no sign of her. I continued to see Caroline daily. She would never speak to me. She hardly looked at me, even when she tossed a water bowl and dried bits of bread into my cage. I didn't have the energy to try to speak to her. The small portions of bread were just enough to keep me alive; the nightly ravages of my body always depleted every single bit of energy I had.

I started having thoughts about death. Similar thoughts had crossed my mind during the early days out on the trail, but once I had become used to life as a sex slave, I never again thought about dying. Not by my own hand, anyway. The threat of death by disease, captor, or some other form of danger when out on the open trail was always a possibility. Now, though, there was no getting used to this. An unmarked shallow grave was far better than just one minute of this living nightmare.

***

I awoke one night to the sound of screaming and shouting from above. One of the voices was clearly Agatha's; her powerful baritone thundered over the floorboards, her distinct accent embellishing each of her words. It didn't become clear who the other voice belonged to until the basement door blasted open and a body was tossed down the stairs. It was Caroline, slumped on her hands and knees, her lavender gown torn and stained, her apron only half on.

Agatha pounded down the staircase, kicking Caroline in the rear once she reached her.

"You will pay now!" Agatha shouted. "I will teach you to steal from me!"

To my shock, Agatha dragged Caroline to the front of my cage, fumbled with her keys, unlocked the door, and tossed Caroline inside.

Slamming the door shut and locking it, Agatha glared in the faint torchlight for a long moment.

"Just like old times, eh?" she cackled, laughing to herself as she pounded her way back up the stairs, locking the basement door behind her.

"Caroline?" I whispered in the dark. "What happened?"

She didn't answer. In fact, despite my near-constant pestering, Caroline didn't say a word that entire first night.

Rescued

A NIGHT OR SO LATER, after Caroline was tossed back inside the cage, her lavender gown missing, her body completely naked, she curled into a ball and began to cry. In the dark, I found her, and wrapped my body over hers. I lay with her for at least an hour, petting her hair and riding the motion of her heaving sobs. Finally, she managed to whisper my name.

"Meredith. Why are you being kind to me?"

"You're my sister, Caroline," I whispered in return. "I am always there for my sisters."

Her sobbing amplified. It was clear she had been moved by what I said. Even I was surprised at my response. Just a day or so ago, I wanted nothing more than to bash Caroline's head against the side of the cage, but now, with her naked and broken on the cage floor beside me, any feelings of revenge or hatred were replaced with silent understanding.

The next morning, another rumble occurred upstairs. This time, gunfire could be heard blasting through the house. The girls above screamed and scrambled about. There were several loud slams and thuds before the rattling keys unlocked the basement door and a pair of footsteps descended into the dark.

"Caroline?" a familiar voice whispered.

"Paco?" Caroline replied, lifting her body from the ground.

The keys rattled and the voice drew closer.

"I am here, darling. Please, I am here.'"

Without ever lighting one of the wall torches, the short man opened the cage door and located Caroline. He pulled her into the darkness, and just as I started to follow, he slammed the door shut, causing the cold steel to thud against my skull.

I saw stars and fell to the floor.

The New Regime

T HE SLAVERY CONTINUED. NIGHT after night, the short man, Paco, would appear in the darkness with a group of paying clients. The same sick routines went on per usual. I never saw Agatha again, and, of course, there was no one for me to ask where she was. Paco provided our food and water for the first few days before Caroline reappeared, again dressed in a beautiful gown. She swept through the basement as if she hadn't just been locked down here herself just days prior. She tossed the breadcrumbs and filled the water bowls. I called out to her when she neared my cage.

"Caroline," I said firmly. "How can you leave me down here? What's going on? Agatha is gone? What happened? Did Paco kill her? Was it because she put you down here? Please, have him free me."

Caroline refused to look at me. She hesitated for a moment when I first called her name, but quickly resumed her feeding duties. She completed her rounds and returned upstairs, locking the basement door behind her.

Whatever had occurred up there, it was clear that Paco was now in charge, and his wife, Caroline, worked right by his side.

Beth Returns

SEVERAL DAYS PASSED AND still no sign of Agatha. Paco was just as vicious. He would snatch us from our cages, always with Caroline's assistance, and slam us over the wooden table even harder than Agatha had done. I started to recognize the sound of some of the men's voices. It seemed this elite group was limited, with the same cycle of men returning every few days.

Then, late one night, Beth reappeared, the first time I had seen her in weeks.

"Shh," she whispered the moment she saw me wake and recognize her. She had a small torch; her eyes were wide and fearful. She fumbled with the keys in her hand, desperate to locate the one that would unlock my cage. Just as she managed to find it and slip it into the lock, the basement door thundered open, and several pairs of feet boomed down the stairway.

I saw Paco and Caroline grab Beth. The torch fell to the ground but remained lit. In the faint light of the dying flame, I saw them beat her, strip her naked, and toss her into the larger cage across the way. Caroline grabbed the torch and followed Paco back up the stairs.

The door was locked, and the basement was again silent and completely devoid of light.

Immune

"BETH," I WHISPERED INTO the blackness.

Silence.

"Beth!"

"Meredith . . ."

I could hear Beth moving through the dark, making her way to the end of her cage. I leaned into the corner of mine. In the complete blackness, I could feel her presence as she approached.

"Thank you, Beth," I whispered.

"For what?" she asked, her voice heavy with the weight of tears.

"For trying. For trying to save me."

"What do we do now?" she asked, her breath labored with sobbing. "How do we get out of here?"

"We will," I answered. "I promise you, Beth. We will get out of here."

Hours later, as Beth was chained to the table for the first time, I stared into the corner of my cage, envisioning a way to escape. It was time. With Beth now a fellow prisoner of the basement horror, I knew an opportunity could be possible.

I tried to comfort Beth after she was tossed back inside her cage, but she wouldn't respond. Her hours-long sobbing was clear and distinct over the usual sounds of the other captives. Like the rest of us, Beth would eventually stop shedding tears over the new horror of her existence.

Just as the rest of us, she would ultimately become immune.

Paco's Secret

A FEW DAYS LATER, BETH was finally ready to talk about a plan. Whenever we could, we would both crouch in the farthest corners of our cages, which were only a few feet apart, and whisper our ideas in the dark. We were careful not to let the others overhear. Although our escape would benefit them—I would never leave this house with anyone still imprisoned in the basement—the knowing of our ideas could put us, our plan, and even them in jeopardy.

Together, Beth and I decided that whenever the both of us were taken to the table at the same time—the slave-stacking was still very popular with several of the clients—we would make our move. We could only hope and pray the opportunity would come sooner rather than later.

The nights wore on, and the usual atrocities continued. As I expected, Beth eventually became accustomed to the routine. Perhaps because of our shared experience out on the trail, it was somewhat easier for us to accept this life, Beth and me, more so than some of the others who had been captured or lured off the street.

One night, one of the male slaves had been discovered unresponsive. Paco tried to revive him but to no avail. Despite all the traumatic activity I had witnessed in my weeks, now months, down here in the basement, I was shocked when Paco laid the corpse on the table and allowed one of the clients to have his way with it. For the first time in countless weeks, I felt myself begin to sob. I cried for the desecration of that poor boy's body; I wept from the frustration of the continuous torture. Something had to be done. This needed to be stopped. I became far more desperate at risking everything just to attempt some form of escape.

The nights rolled on, and I was fortunate not to have to take a turn on the table. Beth, as the newest female member of the collection, was taken to the table nightly, sometimes several times in a row. At least a week after the death of the young male, Paco appeared with his replacement. Instead of stripping the boy and tossing him inside the cage, Paco chained him to the table and tortured the boy mercilessly. It did not surprise me when Paco ended the assault with an intense and brutal rape. I remembered the nights when I had witnessed him and Jeremy together out on the trail. It was no secret to me that Paco enjoyed men. I wasn't sure what the marriage between him and Caroline was all about, and I wondered if she was aware of not only his attraction to males, but also his activity in the basement. This was not the first time I had witnessed him do something inappropriate with one of the male slaves. Perhaps their arrangement was one of security and power, or perhaps Caroline was unaware or uncaring as to the side pleasures her husband took with the unwilling men.

A few nights later, Paco dragged another young man down the stairs. From the things the young man was saying before being muzzled by a rag, it was clear that he was lured here by the promise of a casual homosexual encounter. I imagined that was how Paco captured all the boys who had been chained in this basement, both current and deceased. I wondered how it was possible that Caroline was unaware of what her husband was up to.

Hoping to cause some sort of rift between them, I seized the opportunity the next time Caroline showed her face. For weeks, Paco tended to our once-a-day feedings. For whatever reason, Caroline returned to the duty, at least on this particular day. I took my chance the moment I saw her.

"Your husband is having his way with the boys down here," I heard my cracked voice echo in the windowless room. "Just as he did with Jeremy when we were out on the trail. Are you aware of this, Caroline? Or have you become so self-loathing that you don't even care?"

She didn't respond at first; she didn't even look at me. But to my shock, she reached into my cage without warning and clawed at my neck. I tried to move away, but she secured my flesh with the dagger-like grip of her fingernails.

"You're a liar!" she hissed, her eyes glowing in the faint light of the sole wall torch. "He does no such thing."

"Yes . . ." I managed to choke out, causing her only to squeeze her grip harder. "He does. Just ask the boys. Ask Beth. Your husband fancies men. How can you ever compete with that?"

I saw her grit her teeth, her fingers around my neck nearly stifling the awareness of my brain. Just as I began to see flashes of red, she released her hand and stepped back into the center of the basement. She placed the slop bucket on the table and moved toward the larger cage.

"Has Paco touched any of you?" she asked, her voice shaking.

Not surprisingly, the huddle of naked slaves—both male and female—remained silent. I knew they would never answer her.

"Answer me!" she screamed, reaching for something in the shadows. I could hear the moans of pain as she jabbed whatever she had found into the cage. Finally, one of the boys spoke.

"Yes," his young voice confirmed. "He was my lover for weeks. I thought he loved me, till the day he dragged me down here."

"Same with me," another one of the males added. "I thought we were friends. I thought he loved me, cared for me. He was with me many times before he got me down here."

The third male added his similar account. In the dim light, I could see Caroline just standing and staring. I figured she would accuse them of lying and again poke them with her shadowed weapon, but she didn't. I saw her spin on her heels, drop whatever it was that was in her hand, and whisk away up the staircase.

Hours later, there was a terrible commotion upstairs. It seemed Caroline had confronted Paco with the news she had received earlier in the basement. After several minutes of back-and-forth shouting, objects could be heard bouncing over the wooden floorboards. A half hour or so of silence passed before Paco appeared in the basement, a lifeless body dragging behind him. It was Caroline, either dead or unconscious. He peered around the room, perhaps deciding what to do with her.

Eventually, his eyes locked on mine and he pulled her toward my cage. Once again, Caroline was tossed inside, this time by the hands of her own husband, the man who had just rescued her from this very same iron prison just weeks before.

I tried to push myself against the cage door before he could lock it, but was unable. Caroline's lifeless body prevented me from being able to move. The cage was simply too small.

Paco stared for a moment before returning to the stairs. We didn't see him again for days.

I Will Help You

As before, Caroline refused to speak to me at first. She had awoken a few hours after being tossed inside the cage. After at least two days had passed without an appearance from Paco, she eventually tried to communicate.

"Would it matter if I said I was sorry?" she asked, her voice dry and barely audible.

"It would mean something to me, yes," I replied.

"Well, then, I am sorry, Meredith."

"I appreciate that, but you are right, it doesn't matter now, Caroline. What matters is that you help us escape. You know Paco better than the rest of us. You know the inner workings of this prison you have going."

She remained silent.

"Beth and I are waiting for our moment together on the table," I whispered toward her. "When that happens, we will fight back. With just Paco in charge, he won't be able to control both of us. I doubt the men will do too much. They are cowards. The only way they can even be with a woman is if she is chained down."

"It'll never work," Caroline croaked. "He carries a pistol. He will just shoot and kill the both of ya rather than risk your escape.

A girl tried something like that a while back, back before you were down here. Paco shot her in the face at close range. Even Agatha was shocked."

"What happened to Agatha?" I asked, my curiosity over her disappearance still piqued.

"Paco tried to kill her," Caroline confessed. "After she locked me down here for stealing from her."

"Did you?"

"What?"

"Steal from her?"

"I took what was mine," Caroline confirmed. "I'm no thief. She had stolen from me, and I simply took it back."

I didn't care for more detail. I only cared about devising a plausible escape plan.

"There has to be something we can do, Caroline," I continued. "There has to be a way for us to get out of here."

"You can try," she said after a long silence. "I'm fine down here. I'm tired of all this. I'd rather die in this cage than have to live with him again."

"But I thought you loved him?"

"I did," she whispered, her voice detailing her sudden crying. "I do."

"Then why would you rather die here?"

"Because he will never love me as I love him. You were right. I can't compete. He loves men. I've always known it. I heard him and Jeremy making love back when we were out on the trail. I just chose to ignore all that after he told me he would love and care for me. All those months out there, all those men . . . I didn't want to continue to live that way, and the only reason I was allowed to be the housemaid instead of just another one of Agatha's working girls was because Paco insisted. Agatha wanted me to work willingly, or she was going to lock me down here. I wanted to believe that he really loved me, but I know I was only fooling myself."

"We aren't on the trail anymore, Caroline. You could have run away from here. San Francisco is big. There are many places for you to work and earn a living. You don't need to depend on these people anymore."

Even in the complete darkness, I could feel that Caroline did not comprehend what I was saying. My words had suddenly become a foreign language to her. Unlike Martha and me, who never once lost our rage and desire to escape captivity, Caroline and Beth had become completely dependent on the captors. Even when they could easily disappear into the night, they chose to remain. Something in their way of thinking prevented them from understanding and accepting their freedom. It was just a doorway away. From what I could tell, neither girl had been chained nor caged since arriving in San Francisco, not until recently. Despite the massive opportunity, both chose to remain dependent on those who enslaved them, even without restraint and with one of the fastest-growing populations in the nation just outside the door.

I let her rest for the remainder of what I supposed was night. Paco still didn't visit us. The small water bowls had long been depleted, and we were severely dehydrated. I am sure it was even worse for the other prisoners. There were many of them to just one water bowl.

After what must have been a day or so later, Caroline spoke again.

"I will help," she whispered. "Whatever it takes, I will help."

I reached for her in the darkness, pulling her frail and trembling body to my naked bosom. I felt her fall asleep against me, her body twitching as her brain gave way to slumber.

I must have fallen asleep as well, for when I felt myself jolt awake, Caroline's cold and stiff flesh against me had become dense and heavy.

"Caroline?" I whispered, lowering her head into my lap. I pressed my hands over her nose and mouth, desperate to find a breath. Nothing. In the blackness, I moved my hands over her face and upper chest. She was gone, as cold and lifeless as the countless corpses I had seen during the many months out on the California Trail. I felt for her eyes and closed them, lowering her head to the cage floor. This would be it. Whenever Paco finally showed up to feed us or bring clients to the table, I would make my move.

There was no way he would be able to drag Caroline's body from this cage without my escape.

Agatha Returns

Perhaps it was the long bouts of dehydration that had conditioned my body to the water deprivation, but I was slowly feeling my own consciousness fade into the blackness behind my lids. The usual sounds made by the other prisoners had started to fade. Everyone's energy was completely depleted. After what must have been another day or more, Caroline's corpse began to smell, a choking stench that easily overpowered the constant, wretched stink of the basement. Even the dried defecation could not rival what I smelled now.

I had no choice but to lie against her cold, stiff flesh. The cage wasn't large enough for me to lie beside her. I was no longer sure of when I was awake or asleep. In my overwhelming thirst and hunger, I had begun to hallucinate. I saw the long-lost girls of the wagon train. I saw Martha, the Bethels, Ms. Trudeau, even Zechariah. I longed to embrace them. I longed for their familiarity and safety. Finally, just as I felt my breathing slow and my heartbeat settle into a barely noticeable rhythm, the basement door slammed open and a powerful set of footsteps pounded down the stairs. It took every bit of strength I had to open my eyes and turn my head in the direction of the sound. Holding a small torch was Agatha, her pinched scowl softened to what appeared to be shock and even horror.

She muttered something in German before exiting the basement. I was too weak and tired to wonder about her return. Where was Paco? Had he abandoned us here? Why was Agatha back?

I fell asleep with these questions taunting my limited consciousness.

Self-Professed Lies

SOMETIME LATER, THE SAME pounding footsteps jolted me awake again. Agatha appeared in the darkness, lighting every wall torch in the basement. She had with her two of what I presumed were some of the working girls from upstairs. She instructed them to fill the water bowls and slop buckets while she tended to the dead. Her words were enough for me to force myself to full awareness. Still unable to move, I watched in the faint light as the girls did as they were instructed. Each girl covered her mouth, tears of sadness and fear glazing their faces. I saw Agatha pull open the large cage door, dragging several bodies from within. One, two, three . . . I lost count after four. I squinted to see the faces but was unable. I was looking for Beth. In the shadows, I could see the remaining heap inside the cage stir and move. Although the girls were filling the food and water bowls, none of the nearly dead slaves could move to consume it.

"I thought you said they wanted this?" I heard one of the girls ask Agatha. "How could anyone want this?"

"Crimes or depraved thoughts and behaviors warrant this," Agatha responded in her thick accent. "God himself would do the same to these wretched souls."

The girl who asked the question dropped the slop bucket and bolted for the stairs. Despite Agatha's yelling for her to stop, she pounded up the wooden staircase and out of the basement.

"When will Paco be back?" I heard the remaining girl ask. "Where has he been?"

"He's the most deviant of all," Agatha replied without missing a beat. "I am sure he is off lying with other men. He can't help it. He's filled with the lust of the devil."

Eventually, Agatha made her way to my cage. I could feel her staring down at Caroline and me before she rattled the keys in search of the one that would unlock the door.

"I wonder why this one is here," she stated to the girl, who, dressed in a beautiful green silk gown, stared in horror at the torch-lit scene before her. "She was the wife. Poor fool. How could she not know what he really was?"

I heard the cage door open and saw Agatha crouch. "She's dead," she said flatly, absolutely no emotion in her tone. I could feel her moving Caroline's lower extremities, which were still intertwined with mine.

"This one . . ." she said, her gruff voice deepening even further. "She still must pay for what she has done."

I was too weak to move, too weak to speak. It took every bit of energy I had just to breathe.

"Caroline . . ." I heard the nearby girl sob. "Why was she brought here? What did she do?"

"She was a thieving sodomite-lover," Agatha scoffed. "She's awake in hell in a far worse prison than this one."

I felt Agatha drag Caroline's body out the cage door. I rolled my head to the side, my drowsy and heavy eyes slowly focusing on the face of the well-dressed working girl.

As my gaze focused on hers, I could see tears dripping from her eyes. She peered down at me with a look of pure pity. It took my brain several seconds to register what she did next.

Agatha's voice boomed across the basement like gunfire in a canyon.

"Fucking whore!" she bellowed.

I rolled my body over, my face pressed against the cold iron bars.

In the shadowed light, I could see Agatha wrestling with the girl, the girl's green gown tearing and ripping in the tussle. Agatha's face was a fiery red, a few glowing embers creeping around the side of her head. It looked as though the girl had struck her with the hand torch.

"How dare you burn me!" Agatha raged. "I will send you to the fires of Hades!"

My entire being ached as I scooted my hips backward. I inched my way to the corner of the cage. I struggled to catch my breath, the slight exertion depleting my already-diminished energy. The cage door was still open with Caroline's lifeless body plopped against it. With just my arms, I slid my unresponsive lower half out of the cage and onto the cold basement floor. The two nearby women continued to struggle; Agatha's back was now turned to me. My elbows trembled under the frail weight of my upper body. My lungs felt as dry as the dirt-covered floor below me. I continued to pull myself toward where I knew the stairs would be. The endless weeks of imprisonment had mapped out this entire space in my brain through nothing but memory and sound.

I managed to make it to the first step. I pulled myself onto it, the struggle causing me to drop from my elbows. To my surprise, the sound of my head thudding against the hollow wood did not bring any attention. I could hear Agatha pummeling the poor girl in the distance. Step by step, I dragged my heavy legs up each one, ignoring the firing of my brain as it signaled my looming collapse. After what felt like an endless ascent, I finally arrived at the threshold of the house floor, my body now halfway out the basement door.

I turned my head to see a stunned working girl staring down at me. Her face was painted in a brilliant array of colors, her hair piled high, her evening dress clean and pressed.

"Oh my . . ." I heard her gasp. She looked around frantically before moving to assist me.

"Here," she whispered, pulling the rest of my nearly lifeless lower body from the top of the basement stairs.

I started to fade as the young girl dragged me away from the doorway. I slipped in and out of blackness as she pulled me into the kitchen. I gagged on the water she forced into my mouth, the feeling of the liquid both satiating and vile. My stomach was so overrun with acid that the very presence of the water caused me to heave and vomit.

"What have they done to you?" I heard the girl murmur.

Slowly, more girls filled the kitchen. I could hear them expressing their shared shock, horror, and dismay at my condition. Skeletal, emaciated, filthy, and naked, I lay below them on the floor, a pathetic heap of evidence to the hell that existed just below their feet.

"I thought these girls wanted to be down there?" I heard one of them of say. "Agatha said the girls in the basement were into being tied up and wished to live that way. It helped them stay in character for the men who liked the same thing."

The girls' voices echoed and droned around my ears as they found themselves enlightened to the truth of what the basement contained. Most had been told that the girls in the basement were there on their own accord, and others had been told they had been placed there due to some deceitful act. It was clear that Agatha had them all so brainwashed, they simply never questioned the accuracy of what she told them, nor took the time to see it for themselves. Deep down, even if they had suspected otherwise, none would risk defying Agatha and being thrown into a cage themselves. It was better and easier to just take her at her word, as preposterous as it was. What working girl would willingly allow herself to be locked in a cage, never to be released, except for when her time came to be with the men? From what I could tell, they were not aware of the males also being kept in the basement.

I felt several hands on me, a warm, wet rag, and several more attempts to force water down my throat. Eventually, my body accepted the cool liquid, the feeling of its heavenly flow opening my veins and dampening my lungs.

Only when the thunderous pound of Agatha's heavy-footed boots filled the air did the constant chatter of the girls cease.

"Don't touch her!" I heard Agatha command. "She is a murderous whore! She does not deserve your help."

Silence. No one spoke.

"Liar!" a female voice shrieked, the sound piercing to the soul. I moved my head until I could sort of see what was happening around me. Through the innumerable leather shoes and various-colored skirt hems, I saw the girl in the green gown, her hair disheveled, her face bloody, her eyes wide and wild.

"Paulette?" several of the girls gasped.

"The people down there are slaves! Many are dead. This woman is a monster!" Paulette screamed.

In my limited vision, I could clearly see Agatha's face, which twisted in various expressions. It was obvious she was trying to settle on the most effective response. Shockingly, she chose to swing at the young girl, her fist meeting the girl's wide-eyed face, sending her toppling backward down the basement staircase. The girls around me screamed in terror.

"It's true! No one is there by choice," Agatha confirmed. "They are there for the lurid desires of men. There are even boys down there. But they keep this house as your home. They keep the food on your table. Do you think I could give you all that you have based on what you bring in? You girls barely cover the rent, much less the quality of food I give you or the luxury dresses I buy you."

The girls fell silent.

"I keep you alive!" the German woman shouted, her face a mixture of desperation and rage. "You would all be gutter trash without me. None of you could make it out there alone. You need me. You need this. Only the most deviant end up in the cages. Their punishment benefits your well-being. You must be grateful for their servitude. Do not pity them. Do not feel sympathy. Be grateful to God for their repentance and service for your greater good."

"Goddamn, woman, you make it all sound just so believable," a male voice interjected. I could hear the gasps of the girls in a near-unified whoosh.

"Paco," Agatha grunted, her face darkening.

"Thought I wasn't coming back, did ya?" he asked, the movement of his boots vibrating the wooden floorboards beneath my face. "I was just off huntin' for more recruits."

"You are a liar," Agatha retorted. "You were out fornicating with men. You are a hell-bound sodomite."

"And you think you're so damn holy?" He laughed. "Correct me if I am wrong, but didn't you assist in enslaving girls on the trail? Didn't you beat and chain 'em to a wagon? You know damn good and well none of those girls was deviant. Jeremy lured 'em all to us.

They was all just naive, innocent things. They didn't choose any of this. Not like these whores."

I could hear the girls scoffing.

"Oh, shove it, ladies," Paco shouted. "Y'all know damn good and well you ain't nothing but whores."

He turned his attention back to Agatha.

"But those girls, the ones we kept like dogs, forced to do whatever we made them do for months on end . . . they was innocent. They didn't deserve any of what they got, so you can't tell me you are absolved of that. You are just as guilty as I am, old broad. You goin' to hell just the same as me."

For the first time ever, I saw Agatha's stern scowl morph into something pathetic and seemingly frightened.

"I avenge God's wrath!" she shouted, tears of rage and perhaps frustration staining her face. "I am a servant of God's anger. His holy punishment."

"You a greedy enslaver," Paco taunted. "Just like me, you took advantage of the innocent. So, fool these girls all you want. Fool yourself. Those pathetic souls in that basement don't deserve to be there any more than those poor girls we had chained up behind the wagons."

Agatha shook her head. Even in the distance between us, it was clear that Paco's words were shattering the reality she had carved out for herself. Apparently, she accepted and believed her own lies as truth. She justified her actions behind the veil of scripture and religion. She started mumbling in German before making the sign of the cross. She reached for her thigh, but Paco was faster. He shot her right between the eyes before she could even lift her heavy brown skirt to retrieve her pistol. In my exhausted and hazy vision, I watched the most wicked and evil woman I had ever known fall face-first to the ground. The girls screamed and scurried around the kitchen.

"Get outta here!" Paco shouted. "Y'all fired, ya bunch of no good jezebels. I don't need ya no more. I've made my money. I'm going back home to Georgia. I've got enough money to open a supply shop. I'm gonna sell digging tools to the countless fools who think there is still gold to be found out here."

The leather shoes and dresses floated out of the room. I could hear some of the girls still crying and screaming. I closed my eyes as I saw Paco's white dirt-covered boots step in front of my face.

"You was one of'em," he grumbled. "One of the poor girls who didn't deserve none of this. I don't know how that German bitch convinced herself that ya did."

I twitched and moaned as I felt him lift me from the floor. My body was so light, so frail, that he picked me up with ease. Fully expecting to be returned to the basement, I was stunned when he instead brought me to the nearby parlor and gently lowered my stick-like body onto one of the colorful sofas.

"I only came back here to unlock those damn cages," I heard him say, either to me or himself. "I've got a wagon packed, more money than I've ever known, and my daddy back at home to prove wrong. I woulda just headed out, but somethin' about all this just didn't sit right with me. Sure, y'all made me rich, but I just couldn't stop thinkin' how I at least needed to unlock the cages before goin'. Somethin' about just leavin' y'all down there to die just didn't feel right. I guess I felt I at least owed ya a chance to survive."

There was an awkward silence.

"Good luck, ol' gal," he concluded, slapping my paper-thin backside. Still too weak to speak or move, I lay silent and still as I heard him descend the basement stairs. Even from the parlor, I could hear the familiar squeal of the cage doors. Several minutes later, Paco reappeared in the parlor.

"By God, it's like a graveyard down there," he chuckled. "Well, I came back. I tried. I did my part. My conscience is clean. If the good Lord can forgive me for butt fuckin' men, maybe he'll see this as a good reason not to toss me down into the Lake a'Fire. I did try. It ain't my fault y'all practically dead."

The complete ignorance and irony of what he said echoed inside my brain as I heard him shuffle through the house, knocking over various pieces of furniture, perhaps looking for more supplies or money, before he disappeared altogether, leaving behind only a stark and deafening silence.

In my dazed and weakened awareness, the practically laughable excuses both Paco and Agatha disillusioned themselves with in order to continue to enact their brutal reigns of slave captivity and abuse was baffling. Their self-professed reasoning and guilt-ridden lies and excuses were as sad and pathetic as the countless souls who continued to wearily mine the nearby goldfields for a fortune they would never unearth.

I took a staggered, deep breath and fell into the deepest sleep of my entire life.

Alive

I DIDN'T WAKE UP FOR three whole days. When I did, the room around me was colorful and familiar. Only when Ms. Trudeau entered the room did I realize where I was.

"Oh, to see your eyes open again," Ms. Trudeau said, smiling. "You have no idea just how much we were all so terribly worried about you, my dear."

She assisted my head off the pillow, pulling me forward so I could gulp down several glasses of water.

"How'd I get here?" I whispered, my throat tight and completely parched.

"Your friend, darling," Ms. Trudeau answered, dabbing water droplets from my chin. "He was perhaps the most terrified of all. For months, he combed this city. He knocked on doors and forced his way through hotels, brothels, even private homes. He was arrested twice before he finally found you in an infirmary. You were practically dead."

I downed another glass of water before speaking.

"What about the other girls?" I asked, my voice gruff and hollow. "Where did they take the other girls?"

"I am not sure, hon. The whole thing was in the papers. A brothel with girls in cages. Even boys. How dreadful! It puts a bad name to respectable establishments such as mine."

"I need to know if Beth survived," I managed to whisper, my body sore, tired, and weak. "I need to know if Beth is okay."

Ms. Trudeau just stared at me for a moment.

"Okay, darlin'," she cooed. "I will see what we can do. In the meantime, one of the girls is going to bring you up some food. Please eat, hon. You need to eat so badly."

I smiled and nodded.

Although Ms. Trudeau had mentioned Zechariah, my thoughts remained on Beth. I simply would not be able to be at ease until I knew of her fate. Was she alive? Was she at one of the hospitals or infirmaries? Or was she one of the skeletal corpses found lying at the bottom of a cage in that dark and damp basement?

One by one, Ms. Trudeau's girls filtered into the room, expressing their tearful remorse for what had happened to me. Apparently, the local press had really made a big deal of the shocking basement discovery. After Paco had left and I had fallen asleep, someone contacted the authorities and the brothel was cleared out. The horrifying story of captive sex slaves, a table with chains, and the body count of the victims was front-page news. According to the girls, it was all the town was buzzing about, and I, as one of the few survivors, was a local celebrity. None of that interested nor mattered to me. I had only one concern: Beth.

***

That evening, Zechariah arrived. We held each other for a long while, both sobbing in silence. He didn't say too much, but the girls had all told me of his ceaseless quest to find me. After I had gone missing, the local authorities didn't show much interest in the whereabouts of a former prostitute. They had far more burdensome issues to contend with. Frustrated at the lack of help from the local law enforcement, Zechariah took matters into his own hands. Several times, his efforts resulted in physical altercations with home and business owners. As Ms. Trudeau had mentioned, he was jailed twice, and both times, Ms. Trudeau was the one to post his bail. On the brink of starvation and insanity, he was forced to return to work on the fishing boat. The captain had been understanding and patient of his ongoing ordeal, but eventually, Zechariah would either have to resume his fisherman duties or the captain would have no other choice but to replace him. He still reeked of raw fish as he held me in his arms. He had come here every night since he found me at the infirmary, a near corpse. Tonight was the first time he saw me awake.

"From the papers and what I've gathered from law enforcement, I know it was them," he finally said.

"Who?" I croaked, my voice still raw and hollow.

"Those bastards that killed my family," he replied, a fire igniting in his eyes.

"I need to know where Beth is," I stated, choosing to ignore his anger.

"Who is Beth?" he asked.

"She was one of the girls I knew back on the trail. She was there with me. Down in that basement. I need to know if she survived."

I saw the rage in his eyes flicker.

"So it was them, then?" he confirmed to himself. "God, if I could only—"

"They're all dead," I interrupted. "All of them. They shot each other. Dead. Gone. You have to let it go, Zechariah."

I chose not to mention that Jeremy had been shot out on the trail, presumably now dead, and that Paco had escaped before law enforcement had been contacted.

"Please, Zechariah. Find out what you can about Beth."

I saw the fire in his eyes extinguish as he took in my frightened stare.

"I will. I promise."

I closed my eyes after Zechariah had kissed my forehead and disappeared from the room. For the first time in months, I fell asleep peacefully and willingly, my ears now free of the muffled sounds and cries of nearby fellow captives, or the moaning voices of the shadowy-faced men as they took pleasure with the flesh of unparticipating slaves.

For the first time in months, my slumber was uninterrupted and free, a once assumed right that had become a much-missed luxury that I was now tremendously grateful for.

Edward

A S THE WEEKS WENT by, my strength and appetite returned. Soon, I was back to my normal weight, the emaciated corpse in the mirror now a healthy young woman. I resumed my duties as the house girl, and life carried on as it did before I had been captured. Of course, at night, the nightmare of the basement would haunt my thoughts and stalk my dreams. I would hear the sounds and smell the wretched odors. I would see Agatha—her cruel and weathered face stunned and shocked with a bullet hole in her forehead—falling to the ground with a crashing thud. It would all cycle around in my subconscious like some relentless dust devil. I was able to push through the memories during the day, my daily routine of chores now a welcome and much-needed distraction. The nights, though, were the open playing field of unwanted memory.

Soon, Zechariah began to push his proposal of marriage. Prior to my disappearance, he had only mentioned it once, but in relation to returning to Great Salt Lake City. Now, he was content with his work as a fisherman and did not wish to return to the Utah Territory. He spoke of buying a home and raising a family. I relished his ideas and dreams, but a part of me felt disconnected and vacant. I didn't feel I would be a good mother. Too much of me had been stolen, on the trail, but mostly in that damp, dark basement.

Eventually, I accepted Zechariah's proposal, and we planned to marry in the fall. It was now 1853, and the city was busier than ever. Zechariah rented a room at a nearby boarding house, and I saved nearly every penny I made from Ms. Trudeau. I had more money than I had ever dreamed of making. Working for Ms. Trudeau had been the greatest blessing of my life.

* * *

The summer came and went, but I never stopped thinking of Beth. I would visit nearby infirmaries and hospitals, seeking any information I could. I even checked the death registry. Nothing. Zechariah would accompany me, and we would visit the neighboring brothels, both the establishments equal to Ms. Trudeau's and the seedier haunts where most people would rather not be seen. Still, nothing. Beth had completely disappeared, and it lingered with me as strongly as it had the day I had awoken from the hell of captivity.

On our wedding day, we had a small, simple ceremony at the boat dock. On a quaint, grassy hill near the edge of the shoreline, where the grass rolled into sand, we stood beneath a pair of lemon trees and exchanged vows. A local minister oversaw the proceedings. Ms. Trudeau and her girls shouted and cheered as we walked among them, now man and wife.

We spent the night together in Zechariah's rented room and enjoyed our first sexual encounter. We made love six times, each time climaxing in near unison. The taste, smell, and touch of Zechariah's naked flesh against mine was like nothing I had ever experienced. Despite my countless encounters with men, this felt brand new and exciting. Where I had learned to exit my body and allow the strangers to have their way with my skin, I was now completely connected to every single inch of my being, which was aroused and enflamed by the touch of one single man: the only man to ever capture my heart.

The next day, we scoured the city for a home. Together, our money was enough to buy a comfortable house, but I insisted upon a former brothel. It wasn't in the best area of the city, but it was large and held potential. I told Zechariah that I wanted to run a boarding house for girls, the ones who had found themselves in San Francisco, alone and frightened; the ones who did not arrive to be entertainers, wives, or working girls. The ones like me, who had been brought here not of their own accord, but now had to do their best to survive.

Zechariah was hesitant but eventually agreed. He could see it was something I really wanted to do.

Ms. Trudeau gave me her blessing and even donated a large sum of money to the house. Within weeks, word had spread, and various girls of all ages and races now filled the rooms of our new home. Tapping into the knowledge given to me by Mother back in Great Salt Lake City, I trained many of the girls to be seamstresses. We started taking orders from several of the nearby homes and businesses, and soon, our boarding house became a full-time sewing company. There had been a recent influx of Chinese immigrants who opened several wash houses in the city, so laundry had become a small localized empire. What was washed and laundered was now brought to us for stitching, mending, or alterations. We repaired anything from mine-field denim to expensive gowns worn by the city's elite ladies and even the working girls. By the time 1854 rolled around, we were a thriving, lucrative business.

Zechariah continued his work as a fisherman. He would help around the house as a handyman, but mostly, his time was spent at sea. He loved it. It was his passion, and I relished in his delight.

Life was good, and my memories of the past slowly found themselves locked in a tiny compartment of my brain. The sights and sounds of the trail, the horror of the basement, slowly, it all faded into one massive blur that I now had control over and access to. I didn't go there. I would not think of those memories, even in the dead of night. I had grown, evolved, and moved on. I was a happy wife and business owner. I saw young girls thrive as seamstresses or become educated as teachers or nurses. A few of Ms. Trudeau's girls came to live with me. Some had been forced into retirement from the trade, and some had just grown tired of the lifestyle. I saw girls arrive at the house scared, hollow, and broken, and leave revitalized, strong, and independent. We soon became known as the *Gold Rush Girls*. One of the local papers gave us the name in a cover story they ran on us. We had become an essential and valued boarding house and sewing business. People from all over the fast-growing city knew of the girls who had discovered the true fortune of the California Gold Rush: the prosperity of freedom, trade, and independence, which, especially for women, was a wealth far more priceless and valuable than any metal that could be dug from the earth.

***

In the summer of 1854, one of my girls, a beautiful yet self-conscious twenty-year-old named Dorothy, began to speak of her new beau. He went by the name of Edward, a wounded US Army veteran with a lame arm due to a poorly healed gunshot wound. She spoke of him nightly as the group of girls sat and sewed together in the parlor.

My heart raced and my blood churned the day she brought him to meet us. My eyes locked with his, causing a million memories to fill my head.

Edward was Jeremy.

Jeremy

I DIDN'T SPEAK A WORD to Jeremy, besides a casual hello, nor did he say much to me. We both mostly stared at each other, certain that the other knew full well who the other was, despite the time that has passed since the last time we had seen each other. Jeremy, or Edward, as he now called himself, sat amongst the girls and told tall tales of his time in the army and his victorious adventures across the California Trail and in the gold mines, as well as his budding local business endeavors. The girls listened intently and lapped up every bit of deception that dripped from his mouth. Nothing he said was true. Everything was a lie. He was as deviceful, manipulative, and dreadful as the day I met him several years and so many miles ago.

I waited patiently until he excused himself to the alleyway behind the house. Sneaking out the front door, down the side alley, and creeping up behind him as he stood urinating, his back to me, I pressed a pistol into the backside of his skull and whispered close to his ear.

"Leave here and never return," I mumbled in a near growl. "I don't care if you want to spin your lies to Dorothy. It is her choice to be with you, despite not knowing who you really are, but I do know who you are, and I will put a bullet in your brain if you ever show your lying face around here again."

He didn't move. He didn't say a word.

"Understand?" I asked through clenched teeth, my finger squeezing the trigger tighter.

"Yes," he said flatly, his eyes locked straight ahead.

I snuck back around the front side of the house and stepped into the kitchen as though I had been there all along. Jeremy was quiet during the rest of the visit and refused to look in my direction, even when he and Dorothy left for the night. He must have said something to Dorothy, for she moved out of her room just two days later. I didn't question her, and she didn't say too much on why she was going, although she did tell some of the other girls that I was too controlling and she wanted to help Jeremy—or Edward, as she knew him—with his new businesses. A part of me wanted to tell Dorothy the truth about Jeremy, but I knew she would never listen. It was clear he had said enough to her to turn her against me and cause her to leave the boarding house. I could only pray she would soon see through his deceitful rouse and leave him before it was too late.

I didn't dare mention him to Zechariah. I knew Zechariah would go crazy trying to find him if I did. I also knew that if he did find him, Zechariah would kill Jeremy, rightfully so, and would risk being hanged for the crime of murder, despite Jeremy's immeasurable guilt.

Local law enforcement struggled to keep up with the growing crime rate of the city. Groups would form into militias and take matters into their own hands, causing the city authorities to struggle for control. Public hangings were not uncommon, and I didn't want to risk losing my Zechariah to a public display of death and supposed justice.

Weeks rolled into months. I never saw Jeremy again. I soon forgot about him altogether.

***

It was nearly Christmas, 1854, when a worn and weary girl appeared at the front door of the boarding house. I was off making deliveries of the day's mended garments, so I was not present when she arrived. When I finally returned home and saw her, I dropped to my knees in tears. It was Beth. My God, it was Beth.

After she had been cleaned and fed, I stayed with her all through the night.

She too had been taken to a local infirmary after the authorities were informed of the brothel. She was one of only two girls and one boy to survive the basement. The rest had all been dragged away, buried in unmarked city graves. After she was well enough to sit up and feed herself, the infirmary personnel asked her to leave, forcing the young, penniless girl out onto the streets. One wrong decision led to another, and eventually, she again found herself at the mercy of the desires of men. She ended up in a small mining camp some thirty miles or so from the city limits. She was passed around like a bottle of whiskey for weeks before she finally managed to escape. It took her a week or more to make it back to San Francisco. She'd been living near the docks and taking on daily odd jobs for food and water. She had been living on the streets for several weeks when she saw the front-page article about the Gold Rush Girls. Beth couldn't read, but she recognized me in the black-and-white photograph that adorned the bold headline. It took her several days, but she was finally able to ask around and figure out our location. My heart was overwhelmed with joy, sadness, and relief. Beth had survived. Beth was alive. Her life of hell had continued, even after her freedom from the basement, but I vowed then and there never to see her suffer again for as long as she lived.

Zechariah couldn't believe his eyes when he saw Beth. He chalked it up to a miracle and led us in a private prayer, just him, Beth, and me.

It took Beth weeks to recover, but soon she was a bright and vital part of our small household community. Beth took to drawing and became quite good very quickly. Soon, local businesses were hiring her to illustrate their flyers and ads, and the local newspapers even commissioned her for various artwork and political cartoons. She wasn't always sure of the meaning behind what she was asked to design and draw, but she always did so with flawless execution and detail. Soon, her name as a talented visual artist had spread throughout the city and she was never short of work and income.

***

Beth had been there nearly six months when Zechariah had to embark upon a week-long fishing trip. It was the first time in more than a year that we didn't share a bed at night. I feared for his safety and longed for his touch. Despite our constant lovemaking, I failed to ever sustain a full pregnancy. I was still young enough to conceive, but for whatever reason, my body always rejected the baby. I miscarried twice; both times the sight of the purple matter and fluid reminded me of Emma and her traumatic miscarriage at the brutal hands of Agatha. Even though I was never very far along, I would always bury the remains behind the house, say a private prayer for the soul of my unformed baby, and never mention what had occurred to a soul, not even Zechariah.

I kissed him goodbye the morning he left for his week-long voyage. I prayed in silence for his safe return.

During his absence, I shared our bed with Beth. Despite her physical appearance, which was now vibrant and vivacious, Beth still struggled tremendously with her past trauma. Many nights, I would sit with her in my arms as she wept, her tears an attempt to wash away the lucid memories that had been the hell of her existence for so long.

Five days into the week of Zechariah's absence, Beth and I were awakened by a commotion at the window. The room I shared with Zechariah was at the back of the house on the second floor. To my shock and horror, someone had managed to climb the side of the house, perhaps by the trellis, and inch the window open enough to enter.

Beth screamed as she realized what was happening, but I remained calm and silent; I clutched the pistol that had been under my pillow, where it remained nightly, regardless if Zechariah was in the bed with me or not.

We could smell the whiskey even before we could make out the identity of the intruder. It was Jeremy, drunk and stumbling around like a newborn calf.

"Well, well," he slurred, his face swollen and red. "Two of my old whores. You bitches find each other like ticks on a dog's hide."

I cocked the gun and aimed it at his head.

"Now, now," he muttered, a coy smile lifting the right side of his face. "I ain't here to do nothin'. I'm just here to set things right between us. I just wanna talk."

"Get out, Jeremy," I commanded, my voice strong and stern. "I won't hesitate to shoot."

"*I won't hesitate to shoot,*" he mimicked in a girly voice.

Beth and I watched in stunned silence as he fell to the floor. I moved to find him, but the door of the room burst open and a rain of gunfire filled the air. I threw myself over Beth and rolled us onto the floor and under the bed. The sound of our collective heartbeats was loud enough to hear over the gunfire. Eventually, the shooting stopped, and a pair of boots neared the edge of the bed.

"It's alright," a familiar voice said. "It's Dorothy."

Hesitantly, I slid myself out from under the bed. Beth remained in place.

"Dorothy?" I asked, standing to my feet on the opposite side of the bed frame. "Wha—?"

"He was a lying, cheating bastard," she interrupted, her face smeared with running makeup and tears and what appeared to be blood dripping from her swollen lips and down the exposed skin of her chest. Her hair was matted and wild. It looked as though she hadn't bathed in weeks.

"He forced me to be with other men," she continued, her voice trembling, her eyes wide. "He forced me with other women, too. He's a sick man. A perverted man. He beat me and used me. He's been obsessed with coming here and killing you. He spoke of it often. I didn't understand why until he showed his true self to me. If he did to you just a fraction of what he's done to me . . . then I knew he would not only eventually come here and kill you, but he would kill me too."

I was stunned. I didn't know what to say. I just stood and stared at the wild-faced woman, a shotgun still hot in her hands.

I didn't speak a word as I helped her to the basin. I washed her face and tidied her hair. I didn't bother to tell her of my past with Jeremy. It simply didn't matter now. What mattered now was ridding ourselves of his body and destroying any evidence.

The other girls were frightened and curious, but I was able to keep them from entering the room. I told them a drunkard had broken in through my window, so I was forced to shoot. After an hour or so, the house settled, and I was able to secure some large laundry sacks from downstairs. Dorothy was still in shock and frazzled, and Beth refused to come out from under the bed. Alone and exhausted, I stuffed Jeremy's blood-soaked corpse into the bags, along with the shotgun Dorothy had killed him with. I slid the large parcel under the bed, causing Beth to scream and scurry out.

There he remained until Zechariah returned home.

The Bay

ZECHARIAH DIDN'T ASK MANY questions when I finally revealed to him what was under our bed. He had arrived home around suppertime, and we went about our usual evening routine. I didn't even bother to say why Dorothy was back until I had him alone in our bedroom. I told him enough to ease his worry, and we went to work on devising a plan.

Late that night, in the early hours just before dawn, Zechariah and I loaded the bloody sack onto the laundry cart and covered it with a pile of newly arrived garments. We hitched the cart behind a neighbor's horse and headed for the docks. Besides a wandering, drunken vagrant or two, the dockside was silent and empty. We guided the cart to where the fishing boat Zechariah worked on was secured. We transferred the entire contents of our load onto the boat, every single garment.

In silence, we rowed into the vast bay, as far from the dim glow of the city lights as we could manage. We tossed every piece of clothing into the sea, finally reaching the blood-soaked sack. In an extremely careful movement, fearful and aware of capsizing the small fishing boat, we flipped the sack off the side of the wooden vessel, the density of the parcel plopping into the frigid water and disappearing into the black depths below. Jeremy was gone, truly gone, no longer left to poison this world with his devious schemes and lie-ridden evils.

Zechariah and I rowed back to the dock, secured the boat, returned the horse, and washed the laundry cart just as the sun began to rise over the San Francisco rooftops. It took us hours to fall asleep, after we had bathed together in silence, each cleaning the other of the muck and blood that plastered our skin and polluted our hair and fingernails. We held each other in the soft morning light, side by side in our marital bed. We never spoke a word of what we had just done. Never.

The Gold Rush Girls

I SHARED THIRTY-TWO GLORIOUS YEARS with Zechariah. I lost him to a sickness in the summer of 1886. He was buried in a local churchyard. I had found a Mormon bishop to lead the ceremony. Although Zechariah had long abandoned his faith, I still wanted to give him a proper Saint's burial.

Ms. Trudeau died in 1881. She was nearly eighty. She had left me a substantial sum of money, enough to allow me to relocate the boarding house to a much larger location in the heart of the city. Aside from the usual young, down-and-out female tenants, the Gold Rush Girls soon became a place for aging women, outcasts, and childless widows like me.

Through the years, I managed to stay in contact with Martha. A few months after we had given Jeremy's body to the cold Pacific, I received a letter from her by mail. It seemed word of the Gold Rush Girls had reached even Great Salt Lake City. She, like me, had learned to read from the Book of Mormon. Her husband, Benjamin, had taught her to write. It took years, but eventually she was literate enough to finally contact me, and we corresponded for decades.

Last autumn, one of her seven children wrote to me, informing me of his mother's quick yet peaceful passing. I was now the last of the original girls from the trail.

Beth remained with me for the rest of her life. She never married, and she rarely left the house. Nearly a recluse, she produced her art and saved her money. When she died, in 1890, I had her laid to rest next to my Zechariah. The plot on the other side of his was to be mine when my time came to join them, a time that was fast approaching. I was now bound to a wheelchair. I was well looked after by the girls of the house, and respected and revered in the city.

In early 1892, one of my former residents, a young girl named Samantha, came to interview me for the periodical she wrote for. Like many women in San Francisco, she held a career position that would be forbidden to her had she lived on the East Coast. It took several days, but I told her my entire life story. I detailed the many months out on the trail and the girls I had known and lost along the way. I told her of my time with the Saints, the ones who had been brutally massacred, and those who had shown me mercy and compassion; I told her of my time in the basement, and of my many years as both a wife and entrepreneur. Because of the boarding house, my sewing business flourished, with many of the girls opening their own branches in different areas of the city. Through the educational services I had founded, the city was now full of female schoolteachers, nurses, journalists, entertainers, artists, and entrepreneurs, all made possible by the house of the Gold Rush Girls.

The day after the interview, I asked to be taken to the rooftop. I requested to be left alone there. I looked east, the view of the vast city a radiant orange from the west-setting sun.

My mind took me back to the miles out beyond the horizon, the miles of the trail that had led me to my destiny. One by one, the face of each girl I had known along the way appeared in my memory. I smiled at them as they smiled at me. I thought of their names and stories, but never of their often brutal and untimely demises. I envisioned them now at peace and content in the arms of infinity.

As the sun continued to set behind me and the city began to glow from the light of a million wick-lit flames, I thought of myself and how I had persevered, survived, loved, lost, and conquered. I slipped into slumber with a smile locked over my lips, my mind easing from recollection and into the arms of unconsciousness.

On this night, I discovered peace, and alone on the rooftop of my boarding house, I found my dreams bursting with the countless names and faces of the true fortune-finders of the American West: the women of the California Gold Rush.

Craig Moody was born and raised in Pembroke Pines, Florida, a suburban community that edges the beautiful Florida Everglades. Author of the multi-award-winning debut novel *The '49 Indian* and multi-award-nominated and winning follow-ups *His Name Was Ezra* and *The Stars of Locust Ridge*, Craig currently resides in Fort Lauderdale, Florida, with his boyfriend, Gable, and twenty-four-year-old cockatiel, Alley.